# The Potter's Hands

By

Ronna M. Bacon

Verses
Jeremiah 18. 3 So I went down to the potter's house and saw him working with clay at the wheel. 4 He was making a pot from clay. But there was something wrong with the pot. So the potter used that clay to make another pot. With his hands he shaped the pot the way he wanted it to be.

Isaiah 64:8
But now, O LORD, thou art our father; we are the clay, and thou our potter; and we all are the work of they hand.

# *Table of Contents*

# Chapter 1

 *A*ndrew McBeth was exhausted as he dropped down into his leather chair behind his home office desk.  The last few months had been stressful, to put it mildly he thought, working both as a police lieutenant for the county and as acting police chief for the town of Elmton, now that their police chief was dead. He sighed, his eyes searching his desk. There was just too much there, he thought. He shoved it aside to pull out the envelope his friend Amos Knott had sent him.  He hesitated, knowing that when he opened it, it would change his life forever.  How, he just wasn't sure.  All he knew was that for the next three weeks he was on vacation and didn't want anything to do with investigations.  He needed a break.  Lord, I have an idea of what Amos wants.  He's already given me a head's up, and I'm really not sure I'm the one to tackle this.  But if You're the One leading in this, I have to follow You, no matter how I feel, now don't I?

He stood, heading for his kitchen for a cup of coffee, putting off the inevitable.  He stared out into the darkness, then pouring his coffee, he headed back to the office.  He stood, eyes on the envelope before he dumped the contents out.  His eyes caught the photo Amos had included.

He reached for it and picked it up, studying the young woman there, with her red-gold hair and eyes that reminded him of the wild blue violets his mother loved.  What did Amos have to do with her?

He sat, reaching for the documentation Amos had forwarded.  All he had asked was that Andrew read it over, pray about it and then call him with his decision, either way.

Reading through the information, his heart stilled.  How could this be?  In this day and age, how did people get away with this?

He read through the information many times, finally bowing his head to pray, to seek God's leading.  He ran his hand through the dark brown waves on his head and rubbed at his light brown eyes.  Yes, he was tired, but if God needed him to do this, he knew God would provide the strength he needed.

His hand on his phone, he still hesitated.  He knew this was a life-changing event.  He also knew he could not say no to his long-time friend.  He would help, no matter the cost.  Amos seemed to think it would only take a day or so, and then Andrew would be free to continue his vacation plans. He snorted. What plans? He didn't have any, now did he, other than spending time at home, puttering around with the few tasks he wanted to get done. Nothing that was as important as this young woman's life.  He looked again at the information.  Sure, she was his age, 34.  She certainly didn't look it though.

"Amos?  It's Andrew."

"Andrew, my man.  How are you?" Amos' deep bass rumbled through the phone.

"Exhausted, as I'm sure you know. And you?"

"Trying to keep up with the wife and kids.  It's tough at times, what with the way work is going.  Did you get the material I sent?"

"I did.  I've read it over.  Just a question.  Why me?"

Amos laughed.  "I know it would intrigue you and that you would ask me that very question.  I know you too well, my friend. We need someone who isn't from our town or county to come in and find her.  We also need someone who can keep her safe until we can catch the man or woman responsible for putting her where she is."

Andrew sighed. "I figured that much, but I still don't get why you chose me."

"Andrew, I know you. I know your heart. I know you can get in to where she is and get her out without her getting hurt any worse than she has been."

"What more can you tell me other than what you've sent?"

Amos hesitated, Andrew not liking that. "She's in the hands of a gang, Andrew. Word on the street is that the leader had earmarked her for himself. She's been safe so far as he's been in jail. He's due to get out in five days. We need her found and gotten out of the county to somewhere safe before then."

Andrew picked up the photo again, studying it, his heart tugging within him to help. "All right. Tell me where and when we need to meet."

"We're not meeting, Andrew. That would be a giveaway. You still have your bike? If you do, it's the best way to get in and out. I have word the gang will be at Roadie's tomorrow night. It's usually a drunk fest for them. She'll be there. I need you to go in and get her out of there."

"Undercover, did you say? I haven't done that in years."

Amos laughed. "I know you haven't but you were always the best when we did drama at school. You could make people believe you were exactly who you were portraying. I don't think you've changed that much."

Andrew shared a laugh. "Those were the days, Amos, but I don't have the long hair and beard anymore."

"I don't see that as a problem. These guys are not your typical bikers, at least not in looks. We need your help, Andrew. She's cousin to our chief, and he desperately wants her safe. He can't go in, they've kept her too well hidden."

"What the address and what time are they there?"

* * * * *

Saturday night, Andrew parked his motorcycle behind Roadie's and pulled off his helmet. He searched the area, not seeing anything that caused concern. He sighed, not really wanting to walk into the bar, but knowing he had to. He had dressed in tattered jeans and a tight T-shirt, not quite sure how to go undercover any more.

He pushed the door open, pausing as the smoke sent tears to his eyes and the smell of liquor curdled his stomach. Squinting, he looked around, then saw her, seated at a table at the back, her eyes downcast. There was only one man with her that Andrew could see. Then he noticed the table of men just off to the side and knew they were all together. He made his way to a table behind them, asking for a soft drink when the waitress approached. She shook her head, knowing the tips wouldn't be there from him.

Andrew waited, patience wearing thin at the conversation and drunkenness around him. Then, he saw his opportunity. She had risen and headed back towards the facilities, the man with her watching her walk away before turning around to his drink. Andrew waited, then rose, heading the same way. As she touched the door to the washroom, Andrew caught her arm, a hand over her mouth and pulled her with him towards the rear exit, eyes searching behind him. He wondered at the lack of fight she showed.

Out into the fresh air, he pulled her towards his bike. When she just stood beside it, he pulled on a leather jacket he had stashed in the saddle bags swept her hair up under the helmet he fastened on her. When she didn't move, he shoved her onto it and then slid onto the seat, his helmet in place.  Gunning the motor, he sped from the area, eyes watchful. He heard the door they had come through bang open and yells echo through the night. He had to get away before they caught up with him.  That was a given.  He wouldn't make it out alive, he knew, if they caught up to him and he feared what they would do to the lady.

Thank you, Lord, he thought, we got away from there.  He stopped a short time later, realizing that she wasn't holding on to him, and reaching for her hands, pulled them around him, making her clutch at his shirt.

He turned, searching the area he had come from. So far, so good. He pulled away, heading for a safe area. Amos had given him an address, but Andrew had no intention of going there.  He was heading home, and Phoebe Knight was going with him.  He wanted answers and she was the only one who could give them.

*Chapter 2*

*H*eadlights flashed by as Andrew headed for home. His thoughts whirling, he had no idea what he was going to do. He had done what Amos asked, had gotten Phoebe Knight away from the gang, but now what? Lord, I'm at a loss. He finally pulled over in front on a tired old building, the lights from which streamed through shiny windows. Hitting the kickstand, he slid from the bike and stood staring at the woman still sitting there. He finally sighed, reached for her arm and led her into the clinic.

Doc Ledley, a friend, was filing his paperwork for the night when Andrew and Phoebe walked in. Taking one look at her, he pointed towards an exam room.

Phoebe stood, not hearing what they were saying to her. Andrew spoke, then tilted his head. She stared at the floor, not looking up at all, not responding. He shot a quick look at Doc, then lifted her to sit on the stretcher.

12

Doc finally stood back and studied Phoebe before turning to Andrew.

"I don't know where you found her, Andrew, but she's shut down.  Her back is pretty marked up, and it almost looks as if someone tried to carve something into her flank."  He pointed to the area.  "I can stitch that up and she'll have a scar.  It's the muteness I don't like."

"She's been broken, Doc, somehow or someway."  Andrew's eyes flicked between Doc and Phoebe.  "All I can say, for your safety, is that she's a friend of a friend I was asked to find and bring home."

Doc nodded, knowing Andrew would not say more than that.  "Then, I'll give you some antibiotics and pain medications for her.  If you can, bring her back in about five days and I'll take a look at that area again."  He handed Andrew the medication before locking the medication safe again.  "It's the muteness, Andrew.  That will be the tough part to deal with."

"What would have caused it?"

Doc shrugged.  "Who knows?  More than likely the emotional or psychological trauma she's been through.  She shut down to protect herself.  You've got some work ahead of you, Andrew, to reach her."

Andrew sighed. "Not me, Doc. I'm only an intermediary to get her back to her family."

Doc turned. "If she wasn't safe, then don't take her back to her family. Whoever did this to her will be looking for her again. She's not safe and won't be until you find the culprits."

Andrew nodded, knowing that Doc was right. He pocketed the packet of medication and then reached for Phoebe, his hand stilling as she jerked back from him, eyes still on the floor.

"Gentle movements, Andrew. Talk to her whenever you go to do something. Let her know you're not going to hurt her."

Andrew nodded, then spoke to Phoebe, waiting until he could reach for her hand and lead her once more to his bike.

Heading for his home, his thoughts whirling, he had no idea what he was in for. Lord, now what? I wasn't expecting this. How do I keep her safe if I can't take her home?

He gently led Phoebe into his home, locking the doors behind him and setting the alarm. Now what?

"Phoebe, my name's Andrew. I'm a friend of Amos. He asked me to find you and get you to safety." He watched, seeing no response on her face and sighed. "Listen. I'm going to lead you to my spare room. You're safe here. There's a bath attached, if you want to shower or whatever."

Andrew watched as Phoebe sank to the edge of the bed and just sat. He turned to look behind him, searching for an answer to his dilemma. Seeing nothing, he finally moved towards her, watching as she shrank back. This isn't good, he thought. What did they do to her?

"Phoebe, it's okay to lie down. Here, this pillow's nice and soft. I have a blanket I'll use to cover you." He waited, blanket in hand. When she made no move, he swung her feet to the bed, pulling off her shoes and making her lie down, then covered her with the blanket. Leaving the small light on, he flicked off the overhead light and walked to the door, turning to study her. Her eyes were open, staring straight ahead.

Lord, I'm over my head here, You know. I could use some help. Andrew finally turned, leaving the door open, and headed for his office.

He turned his phone over and over, before he called his friend.

"Andrew?" Amos' voice had an anxious note to it Andrew had not heard before.

"Amos, I have her." He could hear the relief coming through the phone lines.

"That's good. They tried to follow you tonight. I'm not sure if they got your plate number but I don't think they were close enough. How is she?"

"She's shut down, Amos. I had Doc take a look at her. She's been beaten, had initials carved into her. She's broken, Amos, and totally shut down."

"Oh, man, what did they do?" Amos was almost in tears Andrew could tell. "Has she been able to tell you anything?"

"That's the thing of it, Amos. She's not talking at all. Doc called it selective mutism, that emotional or psychological trauma likely did this to her. He has no idea how long it will last for."

There was silence on the phone before Amos spoke. "We've just gotten word the leader has put out a hit on her. How do we keep her safe? We can't bring her back here."

"No, you can't. She can stay here for a couple of days while we figure it out."

"Listen, Andrew. I've had dealings with some who have been through this. It may be you'll be the only one she'll trust."

"I get that, Amos. Let's sleep on it and touch base in the morning."

"Sounds like a plan. Okay, take care of our lady, Andrew."

* * * * *

Andrew rose from the couch in the living room early the next morning, shaking out his blanket then folding it. He had wanted to stay close to Phoebe. He stopped at her doorway, glad she had finally closed her eyes and slept. He turned, heading for the third bedroom and the dresser there. His sister had left some clothes the last time she had visited and just maybe they would fit Phoebe. He pulled out a few items, then headed back to where she slept. He quietly entered, dropped the clothes on the chair, and stood, his eyes thoughtful but his mind racing. He sighed, knowing he wouldn't have answers today.

Coffee cup in hand, he stood on his deck, enjoying the coolness of the morning, the sounds of the birds awakening, and the scent of the flowers his sister had insisted he needed in his garden.  He smiled.  Angela knew how to take care of him.  His thoughts in the past, he sipped at his coffee.  When he turned, Phoebe stood in the doorway, her eyes still downcast, but she had changed to some of Angela's clothes and her hair was wet.  Good, he thought.

"Good morning, Phoebe.  Do you want to come out or would you like some breakfast?  I have coffee or tea or even just water, whichever you prefer."  Head tilted, he watched as she stood, no expression on her face.  He stepped cautiously towards her as she backed away from him.  "If you want some breakfast, that's what I'm planning on making.  Toast, scrambled eggs?  Omelet?  No, not going to tell me?  You want a surprise, I guess then.  Here, let's get you sitting at the table."

He set a cup of coffee, a cup of tea and juice in front of her, not knowing which she would prefer.  He smiled as she reached for the tea.  "Here's some milk, or cream, and sugar, whichever you prefer."

He worked away at their breakfast, careful in his movements, not wanting to frighten her.  She just sat, hands wrapped around the mug, eyes on the table.  Setting her breakfast in front of her, he reached for his phone as it chimed.

"Andrew? Amos. How's our friend this morning?" There was a note of urgency in Amos' voice

"She's up, showered and eating right now, Amos." He walked away from the kitchen to a spot he could still see Phoebe but have privacy as he talked. "What's up?"

"They're heading your way, Andrew. I just got word from the street. The informant just called. He thinks they'll be there in about five hours."

"Five hours? Okay, that gives me time to get some stuff together and get us out of here. But to where?"

"I have some safe houses you can use." Amos started to give an address when Andrew cut him off.

"No, I can't use one of yours just in case it's compromised. I'll find something here in town or the county." He watched as Phoebe finished her meal and sat. "I'll touch base with you tonight. We'll need to keep our calls to a minimum, Amos."

Amos sighed. "You're right. The more I'm finding out about this gang, the less I like it. Don't forget, their leader Giles is due to be released in four days."

"I got that, Amos. Listen, take care. I'll watch out for her." Andrew pocketed his phone and then headed for the bedrooms, pulling out duffel bags that he packed with supplies. He turned and reached for the medical supplies he always kept on hand.

Now what, Lord? Where do I take her? His eyes lit on his Bible and he picked it up and rubbed the worn leather cover before sticking it into one of his bags.

The bags safely tucked into his truck, he headed for his gun safe, pulled out his weapon, loaded it and then pulled a box of ammunition from the safe, heading back to the truck and his bags. Returning to the kitchen, he searched for Phoebe, seeing her standing in the middle of the living room. He stared, overtaken with her beauty, but distressed at the quietness and blankness in her stance and face. He cleared the dishes, then walked towards her.

"Phoebe. You don't know me but you can trust me. I need you to come with me. The men who held you are on their way here. Somehow they found me. I want to get you away from here before they come." He waited for a response and getting none, reached carefully for her hand and pulled her with him, tucking her into his truck. He locked up and then slid behind the wheel.

Lord, where to? Where do I take her? I know I have to drop off that paperwork at the office but I can't take her in.

"Bill? It's Andrew. Look, I've got to run out of town today but I have all that paperwork you'll need. Can you meet me at Jonesy's? Fifteen? Good."

Bill Buckley watched as Andrew walked towards him, his briefcase in his hand. Looking towards Andrew's truck, he frowned. Who was the lady? He knew Andrew wouldn't say unless he wanted to.

"Bill, thanks for meeting me. How's it going?"

"I can't wait until you're back." Bill grinned at Andrew. "What's up?"

"I'm not quite sure, Bill. The lady is my truck? I was asked to pull her out of a situation and now the men are after her." He sighed. "I know what you're going to say and don't. I never expected to be in this situation."

Bill shook his head. "Maybe it's a good thing? Here, let me take your paperwork and you can head out."

"Thanks, Bill. Stay close to your phone. I may need your help. And if you can keep an eye on my place for me, I'd appreciate it."

Bill nodded, now understanding that Andrew was going on the run. "How else can I help?"

"Prayers, Bill. I can't talk to the lady as she's not speaking. Long story there. Thanks again."

Bill watched as Andrew walked way, not knowing when he would see his friend and superior again. Lord, protect him.

*Chapter 3*

$\mathscr{P}$hoebe Knight was terrified, more terrified than she had ever been, and she couldn't articulate that. Who was this man who now had her in his control? He seemed kind, had left her alone, fed her, but now seemed just to be driving endlessly around. She stared out the windshield, desperately willing her voice to work, to ask, to talk, but the words just bottled up and won't come out. Tears of fear trickled down her face but she refused to move to wipe them away, to give her captor the satisfaction of seeing that.

She felt the truck stop, and then a hand reached into her line of sight, a handkerchief in it. She stared at it, not sure what was happening. Then the hand moved and she felt her face gently touched with the cloth, the tears wiped away. She finally heard him speak.

"It's okay, Phoebe. It's okay to cry. I know you're frightened. You don't know me and of course you would be. Amos asked me to find you and help you. That's what I'm trying to do." His baritone voice seemed to wrap her in warmth and comfort.

She finally leant back against the seat and felt the handkerchief carefully placed in her hand and her hand closed around it. She waited for him to continue, but the truck didn't move. She snuck a peak at him, her fear lessening as she took in his looks and demeanour.

"I'm not going to hurt you, Phoebe. I just want to help you." The man kept his eyes looking ahead, not looking at her. "I need to find somewhere you'll be safe, and I'm not sure where. Okay, Lord, where now? The church, You think? Okay, we'll head there. Maybe Silas will have an idea of where we can go."

Phoebe started a bit. The man prayed? The other men didn't. They only used that name as a curse word. She watched as he pulled into a church parking lot, her eyes taking in the white siding and steeple. She waited, not quite sure what was up.

Andrew opened her door and waited, finally reaching for her hand and helping her from the truck. He kept her hand grasped close in his. He sensed a loosening of her body, a lessening of her fright perhaps, and didn't want to do anything that would harm that or cause her to retreat once more.

Silas Peters, the pastor, looked up from the front of the church and then walked towards Andrew, hand extended.

"Andrew. Good to see you." He tilted his head to look at Phoebe, then at Andrew.

"Silas, it's always good to have time to talk with a friend. I need some help. Can we sit?"

Silas pointed to the pews, Andrew leading Phoebe to a pew and then sitting beside her

"Silas, I've become part of a situation that I need some help with. This is Phoebe Knight. I rescued her last night from a gang but I need to find some way to keep her safe."

"And you've come to me for help?" Silas caught the tone in Andrew's voice, one he had never heard before.

Andrew sighed. "I did. Phoebe's life is in danger. I won't go into the details, but suffice it to say, I need to hide her somewhere. My home has been found."

"And that means your vehicle as well, I would assume."

Andrew nodded. "You know how it goes. You were on the force for a while before God led you here."

Silas studied the young woman sitting beside Andrew, her eyes still downcast. "And what does Phoebe want to do?"

"That's the thing, Silas. Whatever they put her through caused what mutism, the doctor said. She can't get her words out. He thinks it's just temporary but until them, we stuck."

Silas held up a finger and stood. "I'll be right back." When he returned, he handed Phoebe a pen and notepad. "My grandmother was mute. She knew sign language, but found it quicker to write. Phoebe, feel free to tell us what you want to do. I'm suspected Andrew isn't taking you home because of the danger?"

Andrew nodded. "That's it." His phone chimed and he looked at it. "Excuse me, Silas. I need to speak with Amos."

Silas watched Andrew walk away, then turned his attention back to Phoebe, who by this time was throwing quick glances at him.

"Andrew's a good man, Phoebe. Don't worry about causing a problem with his wife. He's not married, not yet, anyway." Silas stared at Andrew, then back at Phoebe. Not that, Lord, surely not that. He sat back, his thought racing. "Phoebe, do you have your identification on you?"

She finally nodded and pulled out a small plastic folder from her pocket and handed it to him. He opened it and found what he wanted. "Stay right here. I'll be back. Andrew's coming back to sit with you."

Andrew's brow was furrowed. Amos had called, stating that the men were now in his hometown, looking everywhere for him. How did he get away? And why did they have Phoebe in the first place? He sat, his hand reaching automatically for Phoebe's. She hesitated, then let him take hers.

Silas stood for a moment, watching the couple. Well, Lord, I'm still not sure this is the way, but You are. You did things like this in the Old Testament, now didn't You? Who's to say something like this can't work out in today's time?

"Andrew, what are your thoughts?" Silas' quiet question threw Andrew off.

"I really don't know at this point, Silas. All I could think of was getting her away from my house, and that's not like me."

"No, it's not, Andrew." Silas was silent for a moment, his eyes on the papers he held in his hands. "I have a suggestion, which I doubt you'll take and I know you won't agree with. Just hear me out, the both of you." He looked at Phoebe as he handed her back her documents. "Thank you, Phoebe. I know you're trying to trust and how hard is must be for you. As I said, Andrew's a good man and won't harm you. He'll put himself in the way first. Now, from what you say, we need to move quick and then get you two out of town, right?"

Andrew watched as Silas hesitated to speak. "What's your plan, Silas?" He took a look at Phoebe, noting that her eyes were on Silas. Now, how did he do that, he wondered?

"First, you can't really change her looks. Hair colour, yes, eyes, with contacts you could. But one thing I would suggest is a name change."

"A name change?" Andrew sat back. "We could, but we'd have to find documentation for that and I won't go black market for it."

Silas nodded, his eyes intent on Andrew. "There is one way to change it, Andrew, that doesn't involve the black market." Silas saw the moment Andrew got what he was talking about.

Andrew shook his head. "That won't work, Silas."

"Why not?" Silas turned to Phoebe. "Phoebe, there is one way to change your name they wouldn't expect. Andrew's a good man and will look after you. If you two married, you would have his name and protection. And through him, the protection of the police forces in the area."

Phoebe stared at him. Her thoughts were jumbled, she was that tired. She drew a deep breath, opened her mouth, and then closed it. Words wouldn't come. She was scared but as she turned to look at Andrew, a peace and calm flowed through her. She hadn't taken a good look at him before, but now, she studied him, seeing the strength and power in him, the peace. She finally nodded.

"Phoebe, are you sure?" Andrew's words were soft. "It would be in name only and then we can talk about it after you're safe."

She nodded, then looked down at her hands. Lord, her thoughts ran, I'm not sure of anything any more but You are. I know You're in control. I have no idea why You've let this happen, but You did.

Silas stood. "Okay, I have the paperwork I need from Phoebe. Let's move to the office and we'll get all of it out of the way." He laid a hand on Andrew's arm. "If there was another way, Andrew, I'd suggest that."

"I know, Silas. Let's just get it done so I can find another vehicle and get us out of here."

Silas stood in front of the couple, watching his friend closely, wishing there was another way he could think of. Lord, You're here. I know You are.

Andrew took Phoebe's hand as Silas finished, dropping a kiss on her cheek. He turned to his friend.

"Silas, I know how conflicted you are. But thank you. Now, about a vehicle."

"Let me have your keys. I'll have your truck dropped off at your home. There's an old car in my garage. It runs better than it looks. I've been fixing it up to take out to the races, but it is licensed. Take it and use it." Silas watched at the two walked out of his office and towards the back of the church.

The two had barely disappeared with the doors banged open and four men appeared. Silas slid the paperwork into his desk, then approached them. A few minutes later, Silas lay still on the floor, blood dripping down his face from the blow he had

taken.  They had not gotten what they wanted
from him.

*Chapter 4*

Andrew stopped in front of a store, his fingers tapping on the steering wheel as he studied the store front. He was hesitant to go in, so unlike him. He walked around and opened the door for Phoebe, reaching out a hand to help her out of the car. He watched as she caught the sign for the store and stopped, her eyes searching his face.

"It's okay, Phoebe. We need to do this."

He pulled the store door open, pausing to stare around. What did he feel, Lord, he wondered. Had they found them already?

The clerk came forward. "Can I help you?"

Andrew nodded. "Yes, we need to look at wedding bands and an engagement ring." He caught the shake Phoebe gave her head. "Yes, we do, Phoebe-love. We do."

She sighed, then nodded. She didn't want to do this, didn't want him to go to that expense, but she knew the pastor was right. They had to do this to try to throw off the men who had kidnapped her. And just why they had, she still hadn't figure out. They must have picked the wrong person. She must be the double to someone out there.

Andrew pointed at a ring and looked up, catching the shake of her head. "No, this one, Phoebe-love. It's you."

She sighed to herself, knowing she would lose the battle.

"What's the stone?" Andrew's quiet voice drew her attention.

"It's Blue Iolite. You know, it almost matches her eyes." The woman stared between the two.

"It does. That's the one. Does it fit, Phoebe-love?" Andrew slid the ring onto her finger, finding it a perfect fit.

Two wedding bands later, he led her from the store and tucked her back into the car. He stood, eyes scanning the area, the hair on the back of his neck raised. Someone was watching them, and it wasn't good.

Andrew slid behind the wheel and then pulled out his phone. Amos had been trying to reach him.

"Andrew?  Where are you?"  Amos' voice had a quality Andrew hadn't heard before.

"Why?"  Andrew was not about to tell anyone where they were.

"I heard Silas was hurt.  He's okay, but they were looking for you at the church.  Why on earth did you go there?"

Andrew remained silent.  "Amos, I'm going to forget you asked that.  From now on, this phone is turned off.  If I need to call you, I'll find a payphone.  Someone's tracking us and I have no idea why, unless it's through our phones."

"Andrew, don't cut off contact with me.  I need to know what Phoebe is."

"She's safe, Amos.  That's all you need to know."  Andrew powered off his phone, staring at it for a moment.  He had really cut off contact with everyone now.  He sighed. He had to get another phone and get that number to only Bill.

Phoebe glanced at him, a frown on her face, as he pulled away from the curb, watching for anyone who was around them.

"It's okay, Phoebe.  Just for safety, I'm not turning on this phone again."  He reached for her hand, liking the way hers nestled into his.

He finally pulled into a motel, walking into the office and then back quickly, driving around to the last room on the end. He sat for a moment, then turned to Phoebe.

"We'll stay here tonight, Phoebe. Then reassess in the morning. Come on, let's go in."

She stared at him, then at the room, her heart in her throat. She let him lead her into the room, her thoughts racing.

"Phoebe. Look at me." He waited until she did. "I promise. You're safe with me. It would have looked strange if, as a married couple, we got two rooms." He set their bags down. "Now, we can go eat if you want. Then, I'll take you to wherever it is you need to go to get some toiletries and clothes. Angela's clothes are a little big, I think." He flashed her a smile, and she just stared at him.

"First, though, we need to put these on." He pulled out the rings, finding her finger with first the wedding band and then the engagement ring. He held out his own ring, waiting for her to look up at him. "I would be honoured, Phoebe-love, if you would slide mine on my finger."

Her fingers shaking, she did, then looked up at him.  Now, what, she thought?  And why does he call me that?  He doesn't know me.



Late that night, Andrew watched as Phoebe slept.  He needed to talk with Bill and see what he had come up with.

"Bill?  Hi, it's Andrew."

"Andrew.  I'm glad to hear from you.  I talked to Silas.  Are you crazy?"

Andrew gave a low laugh.  "No, I'm not, Bill.  I'll explain it properly some day.  How's Silas?"

"He's got a hard head.  He's fine.  But where are you?"

"Somewhere safe for now.  Keep this phone number just between you and I.  I've turned off my other phone.  I want you to be my only contact.  Something doesn't ring true with what's going on, and I'm not sure who I can actually trust."

"I think you're wise.  I know Amos is your friend, but there's something funky about him."

"What do you mean?"

"I mean that he hasn't been completely honest with either one of us. He's hiding something about Phoebe and I'm trying to track it down."

"That doesn't sound like Amos. I wonder." He turned to face Phoebe again. "I wonder if that's why she's gone mute, Bill. She knows who's behind it all and the shock was enough to do this to her."

"Anything possible." Andrew could hear Bill shut a door. "Now, we can talk. I traced him back to one of the gangs we broke up about five years ago. His brother was one of the leaders."

"Amos?" Andrew sank down. "I would not have thought of that. But it makes sense, doesn't it, Bill? How far was he involved?"

"I'm not sure. I have a friend looking into it, on the quiet for us." Bill sighed. "Are you doing okay, Andrew?"

"So far, I am. But I think we'll have to find new wheels, though, if they tracked us to the church. Amos would be able to find out what vehicles Silas had registered." He grew quiet, thoughts racing. "Listen, I'm going to head to another town tomorrow. I need to get Phoebe checked out again by Doc Ledley, then we'll see where we end up."

"Keep in touch, Andrew. I have your email I can send the information to."

"No, don't do that. Unless. Bill, set up another email with a different name and text me the information and password. I don't want to use my regular email. Use this phone only."

"Got it. Don was in looking for you earlier. He wouldn't say what he wanted."

"Don was? I wonder. He never liked Amos, you know. Tell him you talked to me and I need him to talk to you about what he wanted."

"Will do. I'll call him as soon as we're free. I'm sending the email information to you now." Bill paused, not quite sure what to say.

"I'm okay, Bill."

"I know you are, but it's just so strange. You shouldn't be the one on the run. And you're not one to jump into something like this. Listen, I did find out more information on Phoebe. I'll email it to you."

"Keep in touch." Andrew clicked off his call, then searched for the email. He rubbed his eyes. He was tired and could not see quite straight. He yawned and stretched, then rose to go and stand, watching Phoebe

sleep.  His wife, he thought.  Now how did
that happen?   He reached and pulled the
blankets up tight around her before seeking
his own bed.

✳ ✳ ✳ ✳ ✳

Andrew sat bolt upright in the middle
of the night, his hand reached for the weapon
he had tucked under his pillow.  Walking
quietly, he made his way to the door, listening
to the noise from outside his door.  He leaned
his head against it, relief coursing through
him as he heard the footsteps walking away
and the woman's voice trying to convince the
man she was with that he had the wrong
room.

He turned, his eyes searching the room.
He felt it, felt the evil near them.  He peeked
through a crack in the curtains but didn't see
anything.  He turned, his eyes now searching
for Phoebe before he padded towards her bed.

She had sat upright, fear coursing
through her as she heard the noise from
outside.  Had they found her again, Lord?
Please, I can't go through that again.  I have
no idea why they took me in the first place,
but they had to have had some reason.  She
was a secretary in a factory, not some rich
man's kid.  She survived on what she made,
with little room for extras.  So why?  She

39

shuddered, so glad Andrew had found her. Now, if only she could talk. What was making it impossible for her to do just that?

Andrew sat carefully on the edge of the bed, careful not to frighten her. His heart was taken already, he knew. Even in just two days, she had entwined herself around his heart strings. He had never believed in love at first sight, even though his parents maintained that's what happened with them.

"Phoebe? Are you okay?" He watched until she looked up at him and nodded. "I think we need to move. Something tells me if we wait we'll not make it out alive."

She nodded, then shoved the blankets back, reached for her shoes, then standing, her eyes watchful, trust for Andrew showing in them.

"So, now what do we do? Do we head back to Elmton, my home, or do we head somewhere else?" He watched as she struggled to speak, her eyes filling with tears. He reached and pulled her into his arms, cradling her gently against him. "Ssh, love, we'll figure it out. I have a friend working on it as well. Let's go, okay?"

He gathered their bags, leaving the key on the table, and once she was seated in the car, stood for a moment, looking around.

There was someone out there, and he couldn't see him or her.  He headed away from the motel, eyes watchful.  He had no idea where to head and that was unlike him. He sighed.  Lord, it's Your play now.  You'll have to lead me in this.  For once, I have no idea what to do, other than to know I have to keep Phoebe safe.

## *Chapter 5*

$\mathcal{B}$ill watched as Don Adams, leader of a security team, paced his office, hands shoved into his jacket pocket. He was troubled, Bill could tell, but by what, Don hadn't said.

"Can you reach Andrew, Bill? I really need to talk to him and talk to him as soon as I can."

"He said you could tell me." Bill watched as Don spun to stare at him.

"I know, but Andrew knows the people involved better than even you. I need to get to him and warn him."

Bill picked up his phone and dialled. "Andrew, are you somewhere you can talk?" He heard the sound of gravel under tires and then Andrew's voice came through.

"I am for now. What do you have?"

"I have Don with me. He needs to talk to you, won't tell me what's going on."

"Okay, put your phone on speaker then."  He heard the click and then the echo on the phone.  "Don?"

"Andrew!  What did you go and do?"  Don's voice showed his frustration.

"Why?"

"If Phoebe's with you, you need to be careful."

"I get that, but why?"

"The factory where she worked?  The federal authorities just raided it.  It was a front for drug manufacturing among other things."

"Drugs?"  Andrew shifted in his seat to watch Phoebe.

"Yeah, drugs.  Phoebe worked in the office, not directly involved in anything.  But the word is out that she turned them in and her bosses are looking for her, as is the gang you got her away from."

"Now, that's interesting, isn't it?  Somehow I don't think she did."

"And how well do you know her?"  Don was pushing and Andrew knew it.

Andrew's eyes were on the rearview mirror and he suddenly threw his phone down and sped away from the turnoff he had stopped it. Phoebe grasped his phone and turned to stare behind them.

Andrew could hear Don's voice, then Bill's coming through the phone but ignored them. "Turn the phone off, Phoebe, please. Then pitch it out the window."

She stared at him, then did as he asked. Now what, she thought.

"Somehow, they've found us again, Phoebe. They must have hacked into Bill's phone or the email he sent me. That's the only way." He finally turned into a busy mall, parked, and then pulled her from the car. "We'll leave what we have here. I'll get us some backpacks and more clothes. Then we'll see about getting a ride. When we're somewhere we can talk, I need to ask you some things."

Andrew watched from the mall doorway as he hesitated just inside. The dark truck moved past, going too slow he thought to be just a customer for the mall. He memorized the plate, and then looked around, spying what he wanted. A new phone in hand, he pulled Phoebe with him, through the mall.

"Good, the bus is here. Hop on, Phoebe." He tugged her hat lower on her face and did the same with his ball cap, watching as two men approached the bus, intending to board, but they just missed it. It was them, he thought. How did they know?

Andrew finally pulled Phoebe off at a stop near a mission he had heard about. Could they find rest there for the night? He had kept her moving all day. He pulled the door open and hand to her back, walked them inside, looking around.

The mission director looked up, smiled, and headed his way. Andrew's heart sank. Yeah, he knew the man, had worked with him in the past. Now what?

"Andrew?" Tom Stowe looked askance at him. "What brings you here?"

Andrew swallowed, not quite sure what to say. "Tom, is there somewhere we can talk that's private?"

Tom studied Andrew, then nodded, pointing towards his office. "My office, I think. And who is this lovely lady?"

"My wife, Tom. It's a long story, but I need your help if you can give it." Andrew stopped as he caught the look on Phoebe's face. No, this was not a good idea, he decided. "On second thought, Tom, I think we should go. Sorry. I'll catch up with you later."

Andrew walked from the building, Phoebe's hand tucked tight in his. Now where, he wondered? He looked down as Phoebe tugged at his hand and pulled him with her.

Andrew stood for a moment, his eyes thoughtful, before looking down at Phoebe. No, he thought, this isn't right. This isn't me, to go on the run like this.

"Let's go home, Phoebe." He tugged her with him to the bus stop and waited, his eyes thoughtful. Lord, what did I do? I know You've a plan, but did I step in somewhere I shouldn't have?

Tom watched from the doorway as Andrew and Phoebe disappeared on the bus, a frown on his face, before he shook his head. Something's wrong and I have no idea what or how to help.

✳ ✳ ✳ ✳ ✳

Andrew stopped Silas' car down the street from his house, eyes watchful. He couldn't see anything but he knew they had been there. He finally pulled into his driveway and slid from the car, walking around to Phoebe's door. Her hand tight in his, they headed for the front door. Andrew hesitated for a moment, then unlocked it.

"Phoebe, I need you to stand right here by the door. If anything happens, run. Get to Silas if you can. Here, the keys to his car. Take it and get away." He watched her in the dim light, waiting for her nod before he moved away, weapon in hand to search his home.

Phoebe stood and watched, the keys clutched hard enough in her hands that she could feel them cutting into the flesh. Her eyes followed Andrew as best she could as he moved through the house. She breathed a sigh of relief as he returned, tucking his weapon back into its holster.

"It's clear, Phoebe. I'll need to check for hidden stuff, but for now, we're good." He reached to brush hair back from her face, his hand stopping as she cringed slightly, worry on his face. "I'm sorry, Phoebe. For a moment, I forgot." He dropped his hand, his eyes taking in the fight she was going through in silence before she reached out to take his hand.

He sighed. This is going to be difficult, Lord. How do I get her to trust me enough to loosen her voice?

In the kitchen, he turned from the table she was sitting at and looked around. Something was off, he thought, reaching for the kettle. That was it. The small appliances had been moved around. His home had been searched.

He reached for his phone, realizing he no longer had it. "Phoebe, I just need to get out to the car and back in. Stay here. The doors are locked. I'll be about two minutes." He waited until she nodded, then strode quickly outside, grabbing the phone from the console and then their bags. He would need to put the car in the garage, but he hesitated to do that. Eyes scanning the area once more, he saw nothing.

He stood in the kitchen doorway. How did she move that fast, he wondered, as he watched Phoebe breaking eggs into a bowl and then reaching to put bread into the toaster. He could smell the coffee she had started and heard the whistle of the kettle. He had been longer than he thought.

She turned, a small smile on her face, uncertainty lurking in her eyes. He grinned, bringing a larger smile to her face.

"Thank you, Phoebe-love. This is good." He had set their bags in the bedroom before he had returned to the kitchen. "Looks like you have everything under control here." He held up his phone. "I just need to check in with my detective."

Her eyes widened as he said that. Just who is he, Lord, this man I am now married to? Can he protect me or not?

Andrew caught the look on her face and then his hand ran through his hair. "We need to talk, Phoebe. I'll find some paper and pen when we're finished. You don't know anything about me and I need to rectify that." He watched as she turned away to tend the stove, and then faced him again. "I should have told you before we went on the run, and we likely shouldn't have done that. That's not me. I don't do that, but I just wanted to protect you. I'm a police lieutenant for the county here and have been the acting police chief for Elmton for the last few months."

Her eyes widened and then closed. He moved towards her as she swayed, gathering her into his arms. "Is that a problem?"

He felt her shake her head and then she pushed back from him, hope in her eyes for once. Maybe, Phoebe thought, just maybe he can stop the men, stop the insanity I've been living in the last few months, stop the fear. She looked up into his eyes and saw the steadfastness there, felt his strength as he held her and knew. Finally, she thought, someone who will believe me and protect me.

## *Chapter 6*

*B*ill stood at Andrew's door later that night, waiting for Andrew to answer. He had known Andrew would come home, but it was sooner than he expected. He sighed, really not sure what to expect. He turned as Andrew opened the door, his eyes searching the face of his friend.

"Bill. Thanks for coming. I know you're not working tonight."

Bill entered, his sentence dying on his lips as he watched Andrew. There was something different about him, he thought.

"I am. I picked up the investigation regarding Phoebe. I wanted to work it myself."

Andrew nodded. "Thanks. I was hoping you would, but don't let it derail you from your other temporary duties. Jason's a good one to work with you."

"He is. He's working it as well. In fact, he headed over to Pine City to see what he

50

could find out.  There's something not right with the investigation there, Andrew."

"Didn't think it was on the up and up. Coffee?  I just made a fresh pot."

"Sure."  Bill followed Andrew towards the kitchen, stopping as he saw Phoebe.  No wonder Andrew wanted to protect this beautiful lady, Lord.  Help us to help her.

"Phoebe-love, this is a good friend of mine, Bill.  He's also the detective working your case."

Phoebe stilled, not looking up, as Andrew spoke.  Bill frowned, his eyes seeking Andrew.

"Phoebe, it's okay.  You can look at Bill.  He's my friend and he'll be yours as well.  Please, Phoebe."

Phoebe finally raised her eyes to Bill, who stared, entranced with the unique colouring of hers.  He could see the apprehension and fear lurking there, then a peace as she looked at Andrew.  Okay, what two or three days here, Lord?

"Nice to meet you, Phoebe.  I wish it was under different circumstances.  Andrew, you said we needed to talk."

"We do.  Let's sit in the living room." Andrew reached for Phoebe's hand and when seated on the couch, wrapped his arm around her. "I don't know how safe we'll be here, but I'm not running any more. Phoebe agrees. We need to find these guys and get them to justice."

"I understand that, Andrew, but from what we've learned, it's much deeper than even Phoebe thought." His eyes were on Phoebe's face. "We thought drugs and their manufacturing, but there's something much more sinister and we can't figure out what."

Andrew pointed at the papers on the coffee table. "Read those. Then we'll talk. Phoebe's written out everything she can think of and more likely. She has documentation hidden that we'll need to go and retrieve at some point."

"Phoebe, you worked in one of the offices, right?" At her nod, Bill continued, "Not with the manufacturing portion? What then?"

She was frustrated he could tell, not able to speak. She turned to Andrew and then back to Bill, finally grabbing the pages and shaking them at him.

Andrew gave a quick laugh. "Like I said, Bill. Read those and then we talk."

Bill read through the papers, then went back through them. "Can I mark these up?"

"You can. That's a copy I made for you." Andrew watched as Bill worked away, knowing he would find what he needed and if he didn't would question Phoebe.

"Okay." Bill finally sat back, his eyes on Andrew. "Have you talked to the investigators at all, Andrew?"

"No, I haven't. I'll leave that to you and Jason. They'll not likely tell me much when they find out Phoebe's my wife. From what I gather, from that Phoebe's said, they have fixated on her as either involved or the snitch. She's neither. From what she said, and it's in that statement, she found paperwork mixed in with her own work about four months ago. She shouldn't have had it. She kept it hidden and just watched. I suspect it was one of the leaders there who arranged for the gang to snatch her. That gang had other plans for her." Andrew's eyes grew thoughtful. "We'll need someone to take her statement, other than myself. You're too close to me as a friend, Bill."

Bill sat back, staring towards the window. "We will. I hate to put her through that again, but we'll need to. Jason could but they might find issue as he's a friend of yours as well. Try Lily. She'll do it."

"Good choice. I'll bring Phoebe in tomorrow if Lily's around."

"She is. She's trying hard to get that spot on the detective side."

"She'd be good. Her paperwork and training are up to date?" When Bill nodded, Andrew continued, "I'll sign off on it tomorrow, even though you're acting chief. We'll deal with any flack afterwards."

Bill grinned. "She'll be happy. She thrives on solving puzzles. She'll be a good one to have in the loop with Phoebe."

Phoebe's eyes bounced back and forth between the two men, not quite following what they were talking about. Bill caught the expression of her face and stopped talking, causing Andrew to search his wife's face.

"Lily's one of our patrol officers, Phoebe. We're moving her up to the detective spot. She'll take a formal statement from you. All you have to do is re-write what you have."

Phoebe shook her head, frustration evident. Andrew watched, knowing she wouldn't do that.

"Okay, then we take in what you've written, the originals, and she goes over it with you. How's that? If you remember anything else, then you can add it in her presence.”

Phoebe finally nodded, then yawned, her head going down on Andrew's shoulder as her eyes closed.

“Give me a minute, Bill, and I'll be right back.”  Andrew gathered her into his arms and headed for her bedroom, tucking a blanket around her, before standing to watch her.  A kiss dropped on her cheek and he turned to walk away, leaving the bedside lamp on.

He found Bill in the kitchen, refreshing his cup of coffee.

“Andrew, how are you really doing? This is so not you.”

Andrew nodded as he reached for the coffee carafe.  “It's not, but it is.  I used to help all the girls who needed help in high school, protecting them as best I could.  I guess that's why I went into police work.  I wanted to continue that on a larger scale.”

“But marriage, Andrew?”  Bill was pushing, trying to understand Andrew's reasoning.

Andrew turned, his face blank, but a look in his eyes Bill had not seen before.  “I can't explain it, Bill.  It's like the Lord said, here's your lady.  Protect her.  Take her as your wife."

"I see."  Bill went quiet.  "That's an interesting take on what happened, Andrew. I know your heart.  She's captured it already, hasn't she?"

Andrew sighed, his gaze dropping to the floor, his one hand rubbing against the mug he held as he leaned back against the counter.  "She has, Bill.  From the first moment I saw her sitting in the bar.  I can't describe the look.  Forlorn, broken, beaten down.  They beat her, did you know? Someone tried to carve initials in her back. They were small enough Doc Ledley was able to suture them together."  Andrew's voice dropped away.  "Bill, what do we know about Doc Ledley?"

"He's a friend of Don Adams, isn't he?"

"I know.  Somehow they've been finding us even though we've run and changed vehicles.  There is nothing to track us on our clothes and our vehicle.  I wonder?"

"The sutures?"  Bill caught on to what Andrew was thinking.  "Do you really think he put something in there?"

Andrew shrugged. "It's possible. He wants Phoebe to go back in another couple of days, but I don't think I'll take her there."

"I wouldn't. Let me find someone who you can take her to without alerting him that you have." Bill set his mug in the sink. "Listen, I have to run. I'll have the patrol officers come by more often. One of your neighbours commented about someone hanging around your home. Stay safe. I had someone sweep both inside and outside this morning, but don't take any chances. I want you back in one piece to take over as chief." He turned to eye Andrew. "Any more thoughts on that?"

Andrew laughed as he followed Bill to the door. "Still praying on it. You'll be one of the first to know. If I do, you come too."

Bill stopped, his eyes searching the night sky, watching as the stars twinkled down at him. "You know, I could handle that. I like my work. I like the men and women here on the force."

Andrew watched him walk away, took his own look around, and then locked the door and set the alarm. He flicked off lights on his way down the hall, hesitating at Phoebe's door, before entering to stand watching her sleep.  Protect her, dear Lord. Let us wrap this up quickly.

He turned and padded down the hall to his own bedroom, sitting on the side of the bed, fatigue flowing through his body.  He needed to sleep, but he needed to watch out for Phoebe as well.  Which would win out, he wondered?  He laid down, pulling the covers up over him.

The person dressed in black standing near his back deck watched the lights go out. He had found them.  Now he needed to find out how to get them.

## *Chapter 7*

*A*ndrew stood in his office early the next morning, watching as Phoebe moved through it, studying the awards and certificates someone had placed on the wall, then moving to touch his plants. She turned, a quiet smile of her face, and approval in her look. He stepped towards her, halting before he got to her.

"I didn't put them up. Someone else did. It's not me to boast."

She nodded, then reached to touch his chest. He caught her hand, reading her glance. She withdrew her hand and moved to the couch that was there, dropping down, her eyes on the floor. Andrew turned to follow her, then heard a knock at the door.

"Lily! Good to see you. Come on in and shut the door."

Lily Ellis watched as Andrew turned to Phoebe, motioning for Lily to move towards them.

"Lily, this is my wife, Phoebe." He caught the quick glance she threw her. "Her maiden name is Knight. I need you to go through her statement and clarify it. She may have things to add. Just for the record, what she went through in the last few weeks has taken her voice, for now. So, if you ask anything, she'll need to write it down. I'll leave you two alone. Come find me when you're done."

Lily watched him walk away and close the door behind him, then turned to Phoebe, who hadn't looked up at her.

"Phoebe, can you look at me? Thank you. Now, this is what you've written so far?" At Phoebe's nod, Lily settled herself on the couch beside her. "Okay, so let's get through this, then you can get on with your day with your more than handsome husband."

Phoebe's eyes flew to Lily's face and her mouth went into an 'O'.

Lily started to laugh. "He's all that, Phoebe, and a sweetheart as well. He's well liked by everyone who works under him. You've chosen well." Lily watched as Phoebe shook her head. "You didn't choose him? He did the choosing? Well good for him. He's chosen well too.    Now, your statement."

An hour later, Lily sat back, drained at what she learned Phoebe had gone through. How had she survived, the initial attack, the beatings, the psychological trauma?    She raised her eyes from her notes and then pointed at the statement.

"I just need you to sign that and we're good to go."    She laughed as Phoebe hesitated.    "Not sure which name to use? Then use Phoebe Knight McBeth.  That will cover it all, I think."  She tidied up the papers and slipped them into a folder.  "Now, do you want to come with me or shall I just find Andrew for you?"

Phoebe stared into the distance, distress on her face, then she rose, pointing to the door.

"Okay, it's coming with me then, is it? I'm so glad Andrew has found you.  You two make such a cute couple.  Just don't ever tell him that."

Phoebe shook her head at the teasing. She liked Lily, a professional through and through but with a fun sense of humour.  She would like to get to know her better.

The officers looked up and smiled or spoke to Phoebe who by this time had adjusted herself to looking up.  She needed to get over the fear she had been put through, she thought.  Lily dropped her paperwork on her own desk and then continued to hunt for Andrew.

"Andrew.  We're done."  Andrew looked up from paperwork he had been reading through, sitting at a table in the boardroom.  "Your wife did good, I must say.  So many details she remembered."

"Did she?  Good."  He nodded to Lily.  "Keep me updated as you can."  He walked towards Phoebe, stopping in front of her and reaching for her hands.  "And now, Phoebe-love, what would you be wanting to do with your day?"  His head tilted as she studied his face, then shook her head.

"You're letting me decide?  Okay, first, we head home and then from there we'll decide."  Arm around Phoebe, Andrew walked away, leaving Lily staring after them.

"And they've only know such a short period of time."  Bill spoke behind Lily.

She nodded.  "I would say it's a match made in heaven, Bill.  Now, you wanted to talk to me, Andrew said."

"I did.  Here."  He watched as she opened the folder.

"Bill?  It says I'm a detective now.  I didn't apply."

"No, you didn't, but Andrew approved my request.  Welcome aboard.  We can use your help with Phoebe."  He grinned as she stuttered out her thanks.

* * * * *

Andrew leafed through the mail as he walked back through the house, stopping at a padded envelope.  No return address.  No stamp.  He sighed.  He had wondered when one of these would come.  He detoured to his office, finding gloves to put on before slicing open the envelope.

He stared at the note and then the pictures that had fallen out.  Hearing a sound, he looked up to see Phoebe standing beside him, her eyes fastened on the pictures.

"Phoebe?  What is it?"

She pointed, her finger trembling, at the top one, trying desperately to talk.

"Is he the one who had you kidnapped?"  At her nod, he reached and drew her close, keeping his arm around her, as he used a pen to shuffle through the pictures.  They were all of her, from various dates and places.

"That man?  Do you know his name?" At her nod, he reached for a pad and pen. "Here, write it down.  I'll get it to either Bill or Lily."  He wrapped her tight in his arms. "Just know that I won't let anyone hurt you, if I possibly can.  You're too precious to me."

She shoved away from him, her eyes tracing his face, her face shuttered before she turned and walked away.  Andrew blew out a breath, then looked down at the desk.  Now, what, Lord?  Where do I go from here with Phoebe?  It's so hard when we can't talk with one another.  I can understand that's frustrating for her.

Phoebe hit the back deck, letting the door fall closed behind her.  Her frustration level was high.  Lord, I need to talk.  I need to tell what I saw, but I can't.  Why not?  It's not fair!

She paced the deck, the twilight growing darker.  She was frustrated and didn't know how to handle that.  She missed her pottery wheel and clay.  Walking down the yard, she didn't hear the footsteps coming towards.  Fleshy arms wrapped her from behind and trapped hers to her torso.  She twisted and fought, her mouth open but no sound coming.  The man fought with her, trying to drag her towards the back of the yard.

Her vocal cords loosened and a single cry was wrenched from her body.

"Andrew!"

Andrew had paced into the kitchen, not sure if he should go outside or not. The single anguished scream had him yanking open the back door and hitting the deck on a run. His heart sank as he saw Phoebe struggling with a man. He raced towards them just as Phoebe threw her head backwards and hit the man in the face. His grip loosened enough that she could fight her way free.

Running towards Andrew, she moved past as he yelled at her to get into the house. She spun at the door, watching as he took the man down. She reached for his phone, her fingers shaking as she called for help.

"911. What is your emergency?"

Her voice rough from lack of use, Phoebe finally got the words out. "Please hurry. Andrew McBeth's home. There's an intruder."

"Stay on the line, ma'am. I have units responding. What's your name, please?"

"Phoebe. Phoebe McBeth. Please hurry." She turned to the door and screamed as a dark form appeared. She slammed the door and locked it, backing away, not knowing if it was Andrew or not.

"Ma'am?"

She could hear the dispatcher's voice.

"There's another man. He's trying to get it." She screamed again as the door shook and the phone fell to the floor. She sank into a corner, her knees up and her arms around her head. This couldn't be happening. It just couldn't.

## Chapter 8

$\mathcal{B}$ill watched as the paramedics worked on Andrew, then turned his gaze to the man in the yard. Officers had him on his feet and headed towards a cruiser and jail. The man on the deck was dead from a gunshot wound. Bill wasn't quite sure what had happened. Andrew was unconscious and there was no weapon to be seen. He turned at Lily approached.

"Have you gotten to Phoebe yet?" Lily's question was quiet as she moved towards the door

"No, I haven't. I just got here, but the officers tell me the door is locked and she's not responding."

"I don't blame her. I wouldn't either. She doesn't know them. Let's try."

Bill tapped at the door and called for Phoebe, finally hearing the lock click and the door cracked open. He tilted his head to look at her.

"Phoebe? Are you all right?" At her nod, he touched the door. "Can we come in?"

Her eyes went past him and focused on Andrew. "Andrew? He's hurt." She tried to shove by Bill but he stopped her. "Let me go to him. Please. He tried to stop them."

Bill and Lily exchanged a glance. Phoebe was talking? When did that happen?

"Phoebe, no. The paramedics are working with him. Are you hurt?" Bill could see the bruising on her arms and face. "We'll get you to the same hospital."

She stared at him. "I am going with him, and I don't care if you don't like it." She shot a look at Lily, who had choked back a laugh.

"I'll ride with them, Bill. You can come find me there. I'll get their statements."

Bill sighed, running a hand through his hair and knowing Lily was right. "Do that, Lily. Are they ready to roll?"

Ezra, the lead paramedic, looked up. "We are, Bill. Lily, you're in front. Mrs. McBeth, or rather Phoebe, you can ride in the back with Andrew."

Phoebe watched as Ezra worked over Andrew, her heart in her mouth. Was he okay, dear Lord. She was more afraid now than she had been.

Ezra shot her a quick look and then stopped, staring at her face.

"Phoebe? Are you okay?"

She nodded, eyes not moving from Andrew.

"Phoebe, please look at me." When she did, he pointed to her face. "You have some bruising and scrapes there. We'll need to get you checked out as well."

Her eyes on him, she felt her face and sighed. "I got them in my struggle, I guess. He was not a nice man."

Ezra bit back a smile. "No, he wasn't. Make sure you tell Lily everything you can remember."

She looked at him and sighed. "Yes, I will. It's been a long few days. I just want all this over."

Ezra shot her another look, then turned back to Andrew, reaching to adjust the IV he had started. He looked through the window to the front of the ambulance and caught Lily looking backwards, a concerned look on her face as she studied Phoebe.

Phoebe shifted on the stretcher in the exam room. She did not want to be here. She wanted to be where Andrew was. She only felt safe where he was. She knew an officer was outside her door and Lily was on her way back, but that didn't help.

The physician examining her turned back from the tray she had laid her penlight down on.

"I understand you had a wound on your back?  Can I see it?"  She moved around behind Phoebe and gently touched the area, a frown on her face.  "Did the doctor say what it was?"

"He said it was something cut into me.  But I honestly don't remember that happening.  I remember the beatings but not that."

"Beatings?  Someone beat you?  I can see faded bruises.  There are some stitches down there, Phoebe, but I can feel something under it.  Do I have your permission to remove the stitches?"

Phoebe nodded, then slid to a lying position as Lily entered the room.

"Everything okay, Phoebe?"

"I think so.  The doctor here wants to take out the stitches on my back."

"Lily, do you have an evidence bag with you?"  Sara O'Reilly looked up.  "There's something in here and I think you're going to want it."

Phoebe stilled. "Is that how they found us all the time?"

Sara sat back for a moment, studying the small device she had pulled from Phoebe's wound. "I'm not an expert, but I think it could be. I see no evidence of anything carved into your back. Do you know if they took pictures?"

Lily responded. "Andrew did, but I don't remember seeing anything there either. Does that mean…..?" Her voice died away as she sealed and labeled the bag. "I'll be right back, Phoebe. Bill's here and I need to talk to him."

Phoebe stood, shaky on her feet. "Where's Andrew?"

"The physician is with him. You can't see him yet."

Phoebe spun, catching herself to steady her balance. "I don't care what you say. If you don't take me to him, I'll search every cubicle until I find him. I'm sure it will be very obvious, with an officer outside the room."

* * * * *

Hours later, Andrew stirred, moving his head as he blinked to clear his vision. A hand found the sore spot on his head and he winced as he touched it. Vision still not clear, he looked around and drew a deep breath. He was in a hospital room, but where was Phoebe?

Soft movement to his left turned his head rapidly that way and he closed his eyes against the dizziness and pain. A hand touched his face as another one found his head.

"Andrew?" A quiet voice called his name.

He didn't know that voice. He squinted, and the face gradually came into view.

"Phoebe?" At her nod, he looked around. "You're okay?"

"I am, Andrew, thanks to you."

He stared at her. "You spoke! How?"

She shrugged. "I had to. I had to save you. I don't know how but I spoke to the 911 operator and they came." She touched his face again, laying her hand on his cheek. "I thought I had lost you."

Andrew reached for the bed controls, wincing as he raised the head of the bed.

"They want you lying flat, Andrew."

"That's not happening, not when my wife has made such a momentous move in her recovery." He touched her face. "Are you really okay? I can see new bruising."

"I am, Andrew. Bill has the man who tried to kidnap in custody. The one who tried to get into the house? He's dead. Bill said he'd be by later tonight to talk to you."

Andrew shifted over on the bed and pulled her down beside him, wrapping her into his arms. "Did they say when I can leave?"

"Tomorrow, I think. They just want to be sure you're okay."

"I'm fine, Phoebe. I've been hurt worse playing sports." He nodded at the door. "We have a guard?"

"We do and Lily's waiting somewhere to talk to you."

Andrew sighed, his eyes sliding closed. "I'll talk to her later. Right now, as long as I know you're okay and safe, that's all that matters." His breathing deepened as he slept.

Phoebe watched him for a while, then her head on his shoulder, she too slept. Neither heard Lily enter and stop, a smile on her face as she watched them. She searched and found a blanket, shaking it out before she covered Phoebe.  Thank you, Lord, she thought.  Now, Andrew can get on with his life.  He has his lady.

# Chapter 9

 ndrew watched as Bill paced his living room two days later, Phoebe tucked under his arm as they sat on the couch.  He half smiled, knowing Bill was miffed about something.

"Bill, sit, please.  You're making me dizzy."  Andrew finally spoke.

Bill spun, his eyes searching his friend.  Then he sat, his eyes on Phoebe.

"How come you spoke, Phoebe, when you didn't before?"  He was still not convinced she hadn't been able to speak.

"I've gone over this many times already, Bill.  I've told you.  It's obvious you don't believe me."  She shoved away from Andrew and almost ran from the room.

"That's enough, Bill.  One, I won't have you upsetting my wife.  Second, she's a witness and we don't treat them like that."

Bill sighed, his hand running through his hair. "I know. I'm sorry, Andrew. It's just that I'm trying to understand it all."

Andrew leaned forward, his arms resting on his knees. "I know you are, but hear me well. Phoebe's been through more than we can even imagine, and it's not over for her. She's scared. They've threatened her family as well."

Bill leaned back, his eyes on Andrew. "Do we have someone with them?"

Andrew nodded. "I've made arrangements for that. Now, where are we in the investigation?"

"Not where we should be. The man who tried to abduct Phoebe the other night is not talking, not even to his lawyer. We can't get an identification on him. And the one who died? Same thing. Our theory is that they were imported by whoever is in charge and they don't have a record."

"Or their record was covered up."

Bill's eyes shot to Andrew as he spoke. "Covered up? As in someone hacked into the system somewhere?"

Andrew nodded. "They've known where we are at all times." He sighed as he ran his hand through his hair. "I think you need to investigate Amos."

"Amos? Come on, Andrew. There's no way." Bill stopped speaking at Andrew looked at him. "Do you really think that, do you?"

"We need to cover all our bases, Bill. We wouldn't be doing due diligence to the investigation if we didn't look into him. The owner of the roadhouse, check him out too. Silas is in the clear, as far as I know."

Bill sat back once more, staring at his notepad. "Where do we stop with the investigation, Andrew? How far deep do we go?"

"As deep as we have to. I felt like I was being set up for something. Amos has never asked me to do this before. He knows I don't."

"Then, why did you?"

Andrew shrugged, his eyes going towards the door Phoebe had disappeared through. "She's why, Bill. There was something about her I couldn't say no to. God put me where I could help her."

Bill nodded, his eyes watchful. "We'll do our best to keep your lady safe, Andrew. We all will. You surprised us, with this, but we get why you did what you did.  But doing that made you a target as well."

Andrew nodded, his eyes searching Phoebe's face as she stood in the doorway, finally reaching out a hand for her.  She sat and he tucked her tight against him.

"Phoebe, I'm sorry."  Bill's voice was quiet.  "I didn't mean to offend you.  I guess I just don't know you well enough yet."

"That's fine, Bill.  I know why you're asking.  But just know I don't keep repeating myself, especially if it's documented in black and white.  You have more questions?"

"I do, but they can wait.  You two need some time to recuperate."  Bill stood, waving to Andrew to stay put.  "I'll see myself out.  There's a cruiser parked outside, Andrew, and one will be for the foreseeable future.  I want to make sure you come back to work so I can give you back your job."

They watched him walk out, then Andrew wrapped his arms tighter around Phoebe.  They sat for a while, both lost in thought before Andrew spoke.

"Is there anything at all that you have remembered, love, that you haven't told us?"

She shook her head. "Not that I know of. I just wish it was all over, Andrew. I'm putting everyone at risk."

"No, not really. We'll work it out. We always do. I have a good team working under me."

"What did you mean the other day when you muttered about having to make a choice?" She turned her head to watch his face.

"You know I'm a lieutenant with the country force, I think I told you? I've been offered the position of police chief for Elmton. Their chief was arrested and then murdered. Long story I'll share with you one day. I have to decide by the end of the month which I want to do. No one else, other than my parents, know I have a timeline."

"Which do you want to do?"

"I'm not sure. I've been praying about it, but so far God has been silent." He watched her face. "What are you thinking?"

"I don't know you as well as I should to be helping you make this decision. I've only seen you react with a few of the officers, but you are highly respected here. If I had to make the choice, I would choose Elmton, just for the chance to work with a town and its people."

Andrew nodded as he thought over her words. "I think you're right, Phoebe. This is where my heart is now."

They sat for a while longer before Phoebe rose, pulling Andrew with her. "We need to look at the groceries we have on hand, Andrew. We're running short on fresh stuff."

"I thought we were, and it's too late now to shop. Tomorrow's Sunday and I don't shop on Sundays." He felt a bit foolish saying this, but it was how he was.

"I don't either, unless I absolutely have to. I've looked into the freezer and the pantry. We can make due until Monday." She stopped, her hand on a casserole in the freezer. "Andrew, tomorrow's Sunday."

"Yes, it is." He waited, an amused look on his face.

"That means church." She spun to him, her eyes narrowing. "What are we going to do?"

"What are we going to do? We'll go to church, our first Sunday as a married couple, keeping our heads high. People will wonder, but they know me well enough to know my character. They'll love you, Phoebe. No doubt about that."

"I know.  It's just so sudden."  Tears sprung to her eyes.  "What about your people?  What will they say?"

"They'll wonder why I hadn't found you years ago."  He approached, his hands on her shoulders, his thumbs stroking her cheeks.  "I know you're nervous.  I get that. We'll go in late and leave early if you want. Mom and Dad will want us to go back for lunch with them.  We can do that, or do our own thing."

She sighed, eyes searching his.  "It'll be okay, I guess."

"Phoebe, what about your own people? Have you talked to them?"

Eyes wide, she shook her head.  "I haven't, and Mom is going to have fifty million fits.  We usually talk every other day. Andrew, what did I do?"

He pulled her to a chair and then handed her his phone.  "We'll need to replace yours, but here.  Call your Mom.  Tell her we'll come visit Monday."

"We can't.  You'll be at work."

"God planned ahead for us, love.  I still have two weeks of vacation left before I need to go back.  God knew what was coming."

"But what do I tell her?"

"The truth, Phoebe. We have people watching them, so they're halfway prepared for what you say. If you want me to talk to your Mom or Dad now, I can." Andrew walked away, leaving Phoebe to make her call in peace.

He stepped out the front door, looking around. He could feel the eyes on him, just not see them. Tomorrow, he would return Silas' car and get his own truck back. That would help.

He turned as Phoebe stepped out behind him, his phone in her hand. She stopped beside him, her hands rubbing her arms.

"They're out there, aren't they? I don't want to run any more, Andrew. I want to stand and fight them."

"Then I stand right in front of you, Phoebe-love. Now, did you find something for dinner or would you like to go out to eat?"

"I have a casserole in the oven. Andrew? Can we take some time to prayer? I miss that. I have a cousin who always met with me once a week and it's been three weeks since I've seen him. We would pray through our family and friends. Tonight, I need that."

Andrew's arm came around her as he turned her back to the house. "Let's find out prayer corner, love, and take what we need to into God's presence."

# Chapter 10

The next morning, Andrew watched the man standing in the entry to the sanctuary, his eyes on Phoebe. Andrew could see the bulge from a weapon and didn't like the situation at all. He moved to a seat where he could watch the man, yet keep Phoebe protected. He saw her looking around, her face hard to read. He started as he felt a hand drop to his shoulder and he stood.

"Drew! Good to see you this morning." Simon, Andrew's father, stood there and drew his son into a hug. "Now, you need to introduce me to this lovely lady you're sitting with."

Phoebe's eyes grew round at the sentence, then flew to Andrew's, taken aback by his grin.

"Phoebe-love, this is my Dad, Simon. Dad, this is my bride, Phoebe. Just a word of warning. He likes to tease."

"Hi." Phoebe wasn't quite sure how to address him.

Simon gave her a quick hug, then stood, her hands in his for a moment. "You chose well, Drew. Bringing her to lunch?"

"Yeah, I am. Just don't plan on your twenty questions though."

Simon's head went back as he laughed, then shook a finger at his son. "Your Mom's going to be miffed that I met your beautiful bride before she did."

Phoebe sat, feeling shocked, as Andrew sat down beside her, a grin on his face.

"Hard to take? This is just mild. Don't worry. You passed whatever test is was that Dad had decided to put you through."

"A test?" Phoebe's voice squeaked, then stilled as a shudder ran through her.

"Phoebe?" Andrew sought to get her attention. "Phoebe, are you all right?"

"He's here, Andrew. Somewhere in this building, he's here."

"And so are a number of officers and my friends. He can't get to you."

Andrew led Phoebe from the church before the last hymn had finished. He knew she was at the breaking point and wanted to avoid all the looks and questions. There had been plenty of those already.

"Andrew?"

"Yes, Phoebe?"

"I should be taking something to lunch for your Mom." A slight panic was in her voice.

"No, she won't expect that. She left it up to us whether we go or not. She doesn't care about that. She just wants her family to come." A sudden movement in his line of sight brought his eyes back to the road in front of him. What had he just seen?

"If you're sure."

"I am. But still. There's a florist shop. I'll run in and get some flowers for her. Would that work?"

She nodded, watching as he ran in and out.

"Andrew? You have two bouquets."

"I know. I couldn't not get one for my beautiful bride, now could I?" He handed her the yellow roses, grinning at the look on her face.

"Thank you, Andrew." Tears welled and he wondered what he had done wrong. "No one has ever given me flowers before."

"They'll not be the last, Phoebe-love. I can guarantee you that."

Phoebe clung to Andrew's hand as he walked through the door at his parents, not sure what to expect. She shot a glance behind her, her eyes narrowing as she felt someone watching here. Andrew stopped for a moment, wrapped her in a hug, and dropped a kiss on the top of her head.

"They're really not scary, Phoebe. They'll love you. Dad does, I can tell by how he reacted at church." He stepped back to look at her face, one hand coming up to cup her face. "I know you're scared and you have good reason to be. Until we catch those guys, you'll always be wondering if you're bringing trouble to them. You're not. Dad's a private investigator and so is Mom. They're both armed at all times."

She nodded, her eyes tracing past him to the woman standing watching them. Andrew turned, seeing his mother for the first time.

"Phoebe, this is my Mom, Emily. Mom, this is my Phoebe."

Emily stood for a moment, then came forward, arms outstretched to catch Phoebe into a hug.

"Welcome, Drew's bride. We have looked forward to meeting you for so long. You are truly an answer to our prayers."

Andrew started to laugh. "You'll scare her away, Mom. What Mom means, Phoebe, is that they've prayed for our life partners since we were born. To her, you're God's answer for mine."

Emily swatted at her son, then pointed at what he held. "Aren't you going to give your bride her flowers?"

Andrew laughed as he looked over at Phoebe. "No, Mom. Phoebe insisted we had to bring you something. These are for you, from us."

Emily stood, silenced for the moment, as she took the bouquet of mixed flowers, tears sparkling in her eyes.

"Thank you, both of you. Now come with me, Phoebe. I could use your help. We usually have both the girls and their families here on a Sunday, but we asked them not to come today, just in case you two did. We didn't want to overwhelm you on the first day you meet us."

"Tell me, Emily, are you an aunt?"

Emily stopped, staring at Phoebe. "I am. Why?"

"I've always wanted to meet an Auntie Em and never have. Now that I have, I can scratch that off my bucket list."

Emily started to laugh, then arm through Phoebe's heading for the kitchen, the song from an old but popular movie drifting behind her in her beautiful alto, Phoebe's sweet soprano joining in.

Andrew smiled, then turned as his father approached.

"Now, Drew, that sounds as if your wife and mine are getting along. Come with me and tell me what's going on and what I can do to help."

"Thanks, Dad. I could use your help. I have our team running through it all but you may have resources we can't touch. I can use your prayers as well. What I did, I'm not so sure I should have."

"I know your heart, Drew. If you have peace about what you did, then you did right. Had you met her family yet?"

Andrew shook his head. "We're planning on heading that way tomorrow. I certainly didn't think this would be how I would be spending my vacation time."

"No, it's not but it's what and where you need to be."

$$* * * * *$$

The next morning, Phoebe watched as Andrew paced, phone to his ear. They had planned on leaving to drive to her home, but that looked as if it wouldn't happen. Phoebe sighed, not quite sure how she felt. She wanted her family to meet Andrew, but she also didn't want to bring any danger to them. So how did she do either?

She turned as she heard the mail box rattle and headed that way, stopping to check outside as Andrew had asked her to. Cracking the door open, she reached for the mail, heading for Andrew in his office.

Andrew pocketed his phone as he turned.

"All set to go, Phoebe?  Bill is still working through an angle, but he thinks we're safe to head out.  I'm glad I traded my truck back from Silas."

"Didn't like his stock car?"

Andrew froze, his eyes on her face until she grinned, then shook his head. "You've got quite the sense of humour there, love? That the mail? Just drop it on the desk. It'll be here when we get back." Andrew hesitated. "We don't have to come back today, if you don't want to. My parents have a cabin in the woods we can go to, if you want, just to get away for a while. Not too many people know where it is."

She stared at the floor, then raised her head, nodding. "I would like that, Andrew. Race you to see who's packed first." With that, she flew from the office towards her bedroom.

Andrew stood in shock for a moment, then with a shout of laughter, took off after her. "Not fair. You had a head start!"

The letter addressed in block letters sat on the top of the pile of mail, forgotten. Little did they know they would be followed, that a timeline had been decided and they would not be home again when they planned on coming back.

# Chapter 11

$\mathcal{A}$ndrew reached for Phoebe's hand as he parked in front of her parents' home and stopped her from moving.

"Before we go in, Phoebe, let's take a moment and pray. I know you've talked to your folks, but talking is different that bringing me here. They had no idea when they last saw you what would happen."

She shook her head. "No one did. I talked to Mom the night before, think I headed off to work, and then don't remember much until I woke up at your place. I have no idea how many days went by until you were asked to step in."

"We think about a week to ten days, but we're not sure on that. No one is saying whether or not you were at work. They're running scared there and we're trying to find out why."

She nodded, her eyes tracing his face, seeing once more the strength he exuded, the peace, the wisdom in his eyes. "It's scary, Andrew, not knowing if coming here will endanger them."

"I know, Phoebe-love." He kissed the back of her hand. "So, are you going to take me in to meet your folks, or will we just sit here for the day?"

She laughed as he knew she would, then waited as he came around to open her door and help her out, reaching into the back seat for the flowers they had brought for her mother.

Andrew watched closely Phoebe's interaction with her parents, not seeing the closeness there he expected. He didn't say anything, but he could tell they weren't happy that she had married and that she had married into law enforcement. Her mother kept mentioning a man's name, bringing him up constantly. Her father just stared at him, not interacting much at all.

Andrew drew a breath of relief when they finally walked out to the car, his eyes scanning the area out of habit, frowning as he studied the dark vehicle down the road from where he had parked.

Phoebe waited until he had pulled away from the curb, then spoke.

"I'm sorry, Andrew. Mom just had to do that. She's been determined from when I was really young that I would marry money and that man in particular, just because he's the son of one of her friends. I can't abide him, never have been able to. He's what the kids today call a slimeball."

"Wow, Phoebe. Why don't you tell me exactly what you think of him?" Andrew kept a straight face but mischief sparkled in his eyes.

"Andrew!" She stared at him, then stared to laugh. "Thank you. I needed that. It's always the same when I talk to Mom. Nothing I do is good enough, and Dad never says a word."

"I noticed that. Now, do you want to go home or shall we find that cabin in the woods?"

She stared out the window. "I think the cabin, Andrew. We need to find somewhere quiet we can catch our breath and then talk. We need to work through where we are and where we're going."

"We do, but I can tell you, I don't want to be anywhere but by your side."

She swung her head to stare at him, then nodded. "Okay. So, what do we need to do now? Groceries, whatever?"

"Groceries, yes. The cabin's pretty much stocked all the time with canned goods and non-perishables. Mom does that so whoever goes there has food. She's put the word out that we're at the cabin for the next two weeks, so we won't have any company."

"She does that?"

"She does. We take turns booking it through her, just to make sure we have time alone there. We've done that since Amy got married."

"That's a thoughtful way of doing it. My mother wouldn't do that. She'd make sure she was there."

"How do your sisters handle that?"

"They're well-behaved. They do what she wants, asking her how high she wants them to jump. I've never done that. If I didn't know better, I would suspect her of being behind my kidnapping."

"Your mother?" Andrew had a sudden horrible thought. "Does either of your parents have anything to do with the company you work for?"

She flipped her head to stare at him, horror in her face. "I have no idea. You don't think…". Her voice faded away.

"I hope not, Phoebe, but we need to sort through everything. My Dad or Mom can look into that without going to the police."

She finally nodded, a sadness on her face. "You know, it wouldn't surprise me if Mom did. It's something I can totally see her doing."

"I'm sorry, Phoebe, that what your Mom's like. I can share mine with you."

"Your Mom and Dad are awesome. I can see why you're the man you are. Now, are we being followed or what?"

"I don't think we are, but I noticed a vehicle parked down the street from us at your parents'."

"That wouldn't surprise me, either. It's what they would do."

Andrew watched the customers milling around in the store, sure he felt eyes on him. He couldn't see anyone that stood out but he knew that if things were done right, no one would see their stalker. He shoved the bags of perishables behind his seat and then slid behind the wheel, his eyes searching the area once more.

"Andrew? Is he here?"

Andrew nodded. "I think so. Listen, before we head up to the cabin, let's grab something to eat. It will be close to dusk now when we arrive and I doubt either one of us will feel like cooking."

"That's fine. And you need to call your Dad."

He smiled. "That I do. It's okay with you?"

She nodded. "We need to know for sure. I need to know if either one of them is behind this."

Andrew pocketed his phone as he looked down at the meal in front on him, his thoughts on what his father had said.

"Andrew?"

"Phoebe?" He looked up at her and reached out for her hands, waiting until she had placed hers into his. "Dad's going to work on that. He had already thought of it and had started his investigation. He'll call me when he gets some information. Unfortunately, cell service isn't great up at the cabin, so he's asked if we can come back down here in a couple of days so he can call us."

"All right. Whatever he thinks is best."

✳ ✳ ✳ ✳ ✳

Phoebe watched as Andrew walked through the cabin, then came back to stand on the porch with her.  He turned her to walk around to the back, watching as her eyes caught the scenery.

"It's beautiful, Andrew.  So peaceful."

"That it is, my love.  We spend a lot of time just down by the lake or hiking around it.  That's a green belt or conservation area on the other side.  There are only four other cabins here and we're allowed to stay because we were here first.  We take great steps to keep this as pure and natural as we can."

The chiming of Andrew's phone startled them.  Andrew pulled it out, staring at it, before he answered.

"Bill?  How did you get through?"

"Andrew, I have no idea where you are, but I hope you're somewhere safe."

"Bill?  What did you find out?"

"Whoever it is just upped the ante. There's a contract now on you as well."

"Wouldn't be the first one."  Andrew snugged Phoebe tight to him as he stared around.

"No, but something's different about this one. I've been told a threat was put in the box at your house."

"There was? We left there just as the mail came and I didn't even look at it. You have a key and the password. Go check it out. But don't be surprised if you can't get through to me. Where I am, the reception is spotty."

"I have an idea where you are. Your Dad called. He's running a search for you, he said, and said the same thing. He'll pass on what he finds. Stay safe, my friend."

"You too. Be careful at my place just in case."

"Will do."

Andrew pocketed his phone as Phoebe moved away from him.

"That was Bill. I have no idea how he got through. The reception is so spotty here, we usually don't even have our phones turned on."

"So, what did he say?" Phoebe stared at him, hands on her hips, waiting for the bad news.

Andrew sighed. "There's a contact out on me as well, he says. And he's going to go check out the mail we didn't bother to go through."

"Was there a threat?"

"He seems to think so. But for now, let's get ourselves settled in. If we need to, we can head back to town tomorrow."

Phoebe watched as Andrew drifted off to sleep on the couch. She rose and spread the afghan over him, then sat back down near the fire, alone with her thoughts. Well, Lord, where do we go from here? You've put us together, but I don't quite get why or how. But You do. You have a plan and purpose in all this.

She found her phone and searched to see if she had a connection. She did. Emily had given her the cell number she could reach either Simon or Emily on. She knew Simon was investigating her parents. She sent a quick text, asking they investigate her siblings and the spouses and also the man her mother had been determined that she marry.

# Chapter 12

*A*ndrew stirred, his eyes cracking open as he looked around. He sat up abruptly, the afghan falling away. How long had he slept? He squinted at the windows. It was morning. He rose and went on a search for Phoebe, finding her curled up on a bed, a light blanket over her. He smiled as he watched her sleep, then turned and headed for the kitchen. He needed coffee. Somehow he knew today was going to be a long hard day.

The chiming of his phone startled him. He pulled it out. He had service? That rarely happened here at the cabin.

"Andrew, it's Dad?"

"Dad? What's up? And how did you get through anyway?"

Simon laughed. "God, I guess, son. Listen, Phoebe sent a text last night about some more people she wanted me to look at. Can you talk?"

Andrew stepped outside, letting the door close quietly behind him. "I can. What did she say?"

"Other than the names and the relationship to her, not much. Did you know she asked me to investigate all her family and the man her mother was adamant that she married?"

"No, I didn't. I fell asleep really early, so I didn't know she had been able to even send a text to you."

"She was able to get through, and that's bizarre. You know how rare it is to get service up there."

"So, what did you find out?"

"Nothing good. Her parents are part owner of that factory she worked at. It was hidden in the paperwork. I pulled in your friend who's the title searcher to help."

"Anything else?"

"Be very careful, son. The man who was her mother's choice has ties to the gang you rescued her from."

"Now that makes sense. Amos said they were holding on to her for someone."

"And that would have been him. I'm glad you got her out of there."

"Me, too." Andrew turned as he heard the door. "Listen, Dad, do you have anything else? Phoebe's up and I'd like to get out and about here in the woods."

"Nothing yet. I'll keep digging. I'm going to get some sleep and your Mom is taking over. Stay safe, my son. You're in our prayers. Love you."

"Love you too, Dad." Andrew thoughtfully stuck his phone into his pocket and turned with a smile to Phoebe.

"Andrew?" Phoebe was puzzled.

"I had service. Don't ask me how. That was Dad." He hugged her tight to him as he turned back towards the cabin. "I'll tell you what he said, but how about some breakfast? And then are you up for a hike?"

The man stood watching from the cover of the forest. He had found them, but he had no way of asking for him. His cell didn't have service, so how did his? He turned, making his way clumsily through the forest until he reached the road. He would have to drive out until he could find service, and that wasn't good. He wondered how he had even gotten involved in this, other than for the money. He stopped. That was all that kept him here. He had some thinking to do.

* * * * *

Shifting his pack, Andrew stopped at the head of the lake, searching the area. He could feel someone watching them, but didn't see the person. Phoebe stood beside him, breathing in the freshness of the air.

"This is wonderful, Andrew. You must have had fun as a child exploring here."

"We did. My friends and I had a cave we used to camp in. I'll take you there tonight. But first, let's head over towards that meadow. There's a waterfalls there you just have to see."

"I wish I had had a childhood like you did. We never went on vacations, never went anywhere in fact. My parents were too busy chasing the almighty dollar. Now my sisters are the same."

"I'm glad you're not." Andrew paused, ready to say more, but hesitant to do so. "Come on. Let's go. This is one of my favourite times of the year to be out here. I also need to talk to you about what Dad found out for you."

Phoebe nodded. "I thought maybe he had called you. I don't have reception on my cell this morning."

"It's strange the way it's going this time. Usually we have no service at all. Dad said it's God."

"It has to be, Andrew. That's the only explanation." She headed down the trail behind him. "Okay, so what did he say?"

Andrew sighed, not wanting to broach the subject, but knowing he had to. "Your parents are part owners of the factory you were working in. And the man the gang was holding you for? He's the man your Mom wanted you to marry."

Silence met his words. He almost turned to watch her but didn't. He needed his eyes on the trail.

"Somehow, I knew they were. It just makes awful, horrible sense, you know? And you'll find my sisters' husbands are involved there somehow as well." As the trail widened, she reached for Andrew's hand. "And it doesn't surprise me Ted was involved in the abduction. I've heard rumours about him and what he does."

"I won't let him get near you, Phoebe."

"I know you'll do your best. Now, what about this guy that keeps following us?"

Andrew shot her a look. "You've felt it too?"

"I think I've seen him a couple of times, and he looks familiar. I just didn't get a good enough look to be sure."

"Familiar in how?"

She shrugged. "Just a sense that I know him?" She stopped by the beach and stared around. "Andrew, this is just breathtaking. How can you live and work in the city after seeing this?"

Andrew started to laugh. "It's how I get refreshed, Phoebe, coming out here and hiking for a day or so. We have a good week we can spend out here."

"I would like that, Andrew. I've always wanted to lay out under the stars at night and watch for a falling star. Thank you."

Andrew turned as he heard stones rolling down the trail behind him. There shouldn't be anyone else out here. This was their land. He pulled Phoebe with him into the trees and held a finger to her lips, his gaze on the way they had just come.

Two men lumbered down the trail, obviously not prepared for walking in the bush. Andrew frowned. They were strangers, but why were they here? He wasn't close enough to hear their words, but their actions spoke of hunting Andrew and

Phoebe. Andrew reached for his phone, photos taken and stored away. He prayed they could get back to civilization and use them.

He turned as he heard more footsteps and saw three more men stop on the trail. There was no way they'd get back to the cabin. Gripping Phoebe's hand tight in his, he pointed away from the trail and then led her forward. It would take work, he knew, to outwit these men. He had to find somewhere they could hole up for the day and then move around at night.

Phoebe finally pulled back on Andrew's hand and he stopped, both of them breathing hard.

"Are they the ones that have been following us, Andrew?" Phoebe stared back the way they had come.

"I can't tell for sure, Phoebe. Here." He handed her a bottle of water. "We're close to where I had planned for us to camp tonight, far enough away from them that I think we'll be safe. None of them look like they really know what to do in the woods."

She snickered, drawing a glance from him. "No, they don't. Now where?"

He pointed, before taking a drink of water and capping the bottle again. "Just ahead is the cave I was telling you about. We'll rest there, but it looks as if we'll have to keep moving. I just pray they don't bring in any dogs."

"Dogs? Oh, you mean search dogs. Would they do that?"

"I have no idea, Phoebe, but we need to keep moving."

Andrew stood at the cave entrance, eyes searching the area around them. He felt they were safe for a while, but he knew they had to keep moving, but to where? He checked his phone. No reception. Just when he really needed it too. He sighed, then turned to watch Phoebe. She had dropped to the cave floor, her head down on her upraised knees, her hair hiding her face. This is not how I planned to spend the day, Lord. We certainly could use Your help.

"Andrew?" Phoebe looked up at him. "Are we safe?"

He dropped to sit beside her, wanting to reach for her, but not daring to. "I hope so, Phoebe. We'll need to move, but we may have to do that at night."

"Night? And just how do we do that?"

Andrew shrugged. "I'm not sure. We'll see what happens over the next couple of hours. They would have a good walk to here from where we left them and they would have to know the area to know this cave. It's hidden and as far as I know only myself and my sisters know where it is."

"I guess that's a relief." Phoebe straightened up to lean against the wall. "Andrew, did Silas really mean that on Sunday?"

Andrew rolled his head to look at her. "Mean what, love?"

"About God being a potter and us the clay?" She studied his face. "I feel like that piece of broken pottery right now, or that lump of clay the potter is trying to form and can't."

"It's in the Bible, love. It states He's the potter, we are the clay. He takes that lump of clay and forms it into the vessel He can use. None of us are perfect, so he works with our imperfections and uses us." He paused. "My mom does pottery as a hobby. She's let me do a few jars. It's harder than it looks."

"I'm sure it is. Do you think she'd let me try? I had a wheel when I was younger."

Andrew wrapped an arm around her. "She would, Phoebe. My sisters have done it as well, but none of us have the talent for it like Mom does.  She would be thrilled if you did.”

Phoebe’s attention was drawn to the outside of the cave, and Andrew rose, his weapon in his hand.  He listened, eyes searching the area outside, before he holstered his weapon and stepped back to Phoebe.

“It was a doe and her fawn.” He looked around at the dimming light.  “I think we’ll stay here tonight, and then get an early start in the morning.  Don’t worry, I’ll make sure you have a comfortable bed.  We just can’t light a fire like I had hoped to.”

“Don’t worry about that, Andrew.  We just need to do what we have to in order to stay safe.”

*Chapter 13*

$\mathscr{A}$ndrew roused, his head raising from the sleeping bag he was lying on, blinking to clear the sleep from his eyes. It was pre-dawn he could tell. He rose and crept to the entrance of the cave, listening. His chin dropped to his chest. The men were out there. He could hear them talking. Now what, Lord? How do I get us out of here without being seen? It would be a good time for that army of angels to surround us.

He sensed Phoebe at his side and he reached for her hand, squeezing it. She moved away and he could hear her quickly gathering up their gear and repacking it. He smiled. She could read his mind, almost, he thought, in a way few others than his own family could. He felt his phone vibrate against his chest and pulled it out. Wonderful, he thought. Service.

He read the text from his Dad, his heart sinking, before he turned to look at Phoebe. He knew the information his Dad and Mom had found would be devastating for her.

111

He moved away from the entrance towards the back of the cave, drawing Phoebe with him.  A few quiet words and then they had their backpacks on and were creeping away from the cave.  Andrew knew a lot of trails going through the woods that not many others did, and he hoped one of them would eventually lead them away from their followers.

Phoebe finally stopped, needing to catch her breath.  She pulled out her water bottle and took a quick drink before stuffing it back into the pack.

"Are we safe for now, Andrew?  We need to rest and eat."

He nodded, eyes scanning the area around him.  "I think so.  If we're quick, we should be okay."

He paused, his eyes drawn to the horizon.  Now what, he thought?  He pulled Phoebe back into the forest as the drone of a plane came to their ears.  His eyes sliding closed, he knew.  They were up trying to spot them from the air.

Her hand on his arm, Phoebe spoke. "They're looking for us, aren't they?"

Andrew nodded.  "I suspect so.  Next thing we know, they'll have a drone up there.

We're fine here for now. Let's grab some food and then move on."

"Do you have a destination in mind, Andrew?"

He nodded. "I do. If we can make it through to the river, I know where a friend has a canoe stashed for me. He brought it up yesterday morning."

"A canoe?" Her voice rose. "Andrew, I can't swim."

He spun to stare at her. "You can't swim?" When she shook her head, he paused. "He usually stashes life jackets with it. I hope he has. I won't put you at risk, Phoebe. Not a chance on that happening."

"But what about you?"

"I'll be fine. Are you finished? Then let's move. We need to keep close to the trees just in case the plane returns."

"How sure are you that it was them?"

Andrew took a look at the sky. "Fairly sure. They need to find us and that's the quickest way they have." He paused. "Before we left the cave, I got a text from my Dad. Yeah, I know. Spotty service." He watched her face. "He said your brothers-in-law are involved in the factory as well, behind the scenes. He's still tracking down information. And the man your Mom wanted you to marry?  He's disappeared, so he warned me to be very careful.  Dad thinks he's come to my area looking for you."

"How would he know?"  She stopped walking, horror on her face.  "Andrew, that doctor you took me to.  Did you know he implanted a device into my back?  There was no cutting until he did that."

Andrew spun.  "What?  How did you find out?"

"The night you were hurt, the doctor took a look at my back and found that.  She turned it over to Lily."

Andrew blew out a breath.  "This is just getting stranger and stranger.  I thought we could trust Doc Ledley."

"Obviously, you can't.  Now, can we move?"

He nodded, turning around to walk towards the river.  It would be a long day and he knew they'd have to spend another night outside.  This is definitely not how he had planned the week.  Okay, Lord, I know You're in control, that You have a plan and purpose.  It would be nice if You shared with us.

Late afternoon, Andrew finally stopped. He had reached the river and just needed to find the canoe. They would head down the river in the morning, but first he had to make sure he was in the right spot. He pointed to the shelter of the trees and Phoebe sank down gratefully. She was exhausted and needed that rest.

Andrew finally returned. He had found the canoe and his friend had a life jacket in it. There was only the one but it would do for Phoebe.

"I found the canoe, Phoebe. We'll head out early morning and hopefully get away."

"But it's so open, Andrew. They'll spot us from the air."

He nodded. "I know. It's the best I can do, Phoebe. I need to get us down river and then we can head out again. Listen, eat something and then we'll rest. Thank you for being such a good sport today."

* * * * *

Before dawn the next morning, Andrew had them up and down by the river, fastening the lifejacket on Phoebe. His friend had encased it in plastic and tucked it into the canoe where it would be safe. She looked at him, then at the river.

"We're really doing this?"

He nodded. "We have to, Phoebe. Right now, this is the only way I know how to get us out of here quickly." He turned and searched the area. "I don't think we have all that much time. In you go. Let me paddle for now, okay?"

"Fine. Just let me get my balance and then you can paddle the canoe anywhere you want to."

Andrew gave a low laugh. "That's the spirit, my love."

Hours later, Andrew finally beached the canoe, then reached for Phoebe's hand.

"Just where are we, Andrew?" She looked around, a frown on her face.

"Near Elmton, Phoebe. It's just a short walk back to our home."

She turned. "Really, we traveled all that way on the water?"

He nodded. "We did. Some day, we trace our way upriver."

She nodded, her eyes searching the area. "I don't feel safe, Andrew. And what about your truck?"

"Bill headed up to get it, I think. I let him know before we left that if he hadn't heard from me by today, he should get the truck and bring it back."

She spun. "You planned on us coming back by water?"

He grinned. "I had hoped to. But circumstances sort of forced the issue, didn't they?" He pulled the canoe up and fastened it securely. "My friend will come and get it. You can leave the lifejacket in it."

She turned, her eyes searching the area. "When do you go back to work?"

"In about a week. Why?"

She shrugged. "I'm just trying to think of what I can do to put in time when you do."

Andrew caught her hand as they walked towards town. "We'll think of something, love. I know the ladies have a Bible study you'd be welcome to join. We need to get you a car."

"I had a car, but I don't think I want it any more." She shivered. "Maybe just a bike."

"Not happening, not yet anyway." He pointed ahead. "We can cut through here and get to the backyard."

He paused at the edge of the yard, suddenly not wanting to go any further. He searched, not quite sure about what had triggered an alarm with him.

"Andrew?  Are we not going to the house?"

He shook his head. "No, I don't think so.  Let's head away from here.  There's something there I can't put my finger on."

He finally pulled her down beside him on a park bench, not letting go of her hand. Pulling out his phone, he checked.  He still had some charge left on it.

"Bill? Hi.  Where are you?"

"Looking for you.  Where'd you disappear to?  I have your truck at your place."

"Are you still there?"

"I am.  I just got here.  Why?"

"Search the area and then check inside please. We were just there and something felt off.  Let me know if it's safe to come back there."

"I will.  You two are okay?"

"We are."  Andrew looked around, feeling eyes on him. "I need to keep moving, Bill, and I don't have a lot of charge left on my phone. I'll head back your way."

Bill watched as Andrew and Phoebe walked towards him, a frown on his face. He had found nothing overtly wrong at Andrew's but if Andrew was spooked, then there was a reason.

"Bill?" Andrew's question was quiet.

"I didn't find anything, Andrew, but I'm sure they've been around. I have a tech coming to look around as well."

Andrew sighed. "Maybe it was nothing but after being chased through the woods, I can't take a chance."

Bill spun to stare at him. "Chased through the woods?"

Andrew nodded towards the house. "Let's get Phoebe inside and then we can talk."

* * * * *

Bill walked away from the house a couple of hours later, his mind spinning with what Andrew had told him. He sighed. It was going to be a long night, he thought.

Andrew turned from the door, searching for Phoebe. He stopped at her bedroom door, finding her just sitting on the side of the bed, staring at the floor. He dropped down beside her, not saying anything.

Phoebe finally spoke. "Will it ever be over, Andrew?"

Andrew stared at the floor before wrapping her into a hug. "Soon, I hope, love." He tilted his head to watch her face, brushing her hair behind her ear. "Are you hungry?" When she shook her head, he nodded. "How be you crawl into bed then? We didn't get a lot of sleep last night, and it's been a stressful couple of days." He waited for her to speak. "Not how I planned to spend them."

She nodded. "I think I will turn in. Andrew, can you just hold me for a while?" She turned to him, her eyes shadowed with fatigue and something he couldn't read.

"Sure." He stood, waiting until she had crawled beneath the covers, then lay down wrapping his arms around her again, and pulling her close to him.

He waited as she drifted off to sleep, with every intention of rising and seeking his own bed. His eyes closed and he slept, his wife cradled in his arms.

## Chapter 14

Standing on his back deck the next morning, Andrew stared around.  He could feel the eyes, feel the evil.  Something was different back there, and he couldn't put his finger on it.  He had awakened early, surprised to find himself still cradling Phoebe to his chest, but that was something he would like to do every day for the rest of his life.  He sighed, knowing they had rushed into something that should have waited, but he knew it had been the only way he could think of to keep her safe.  His father would tell him to court her, just as he did Andrew's mother every day.

He turned as he heard the back door. Phoebe stood there, watching him in silence. He reached out a hand and she took it, moving into his space.

"Andrew?"

"Yes, love?"

"You're not back to work today, are you?"  When he shook his head, she turned her head to look up at him. "Can we go clean out my apartment? I would like to put that behind me."

"We can. Do you have a lot of stuff?"

She shook her head. "Just some furniture and personal stuff."

"I can rent a truck, and I have some friends who will help."

She started at this. "But they don't know me, so why?"

He shrugged. "Because you're my wife. That's all they want to know. That's what we do for one another."

She sighed. "I've never had that, you know. Never had a close friend like that." Tears sparkled in her eyes.

"Tell you what. Once we get your place cleaned out and you've met the guys, we'll have them over for a meal. I have four friends who are pretty much newlyweds or married just over a year. Their wives want to get to know you."

She nodded. "When do you go back to work?"

"A week Monday. We still have a few days I'll be home." He wrapped her into a hug. "We'll find him, Phoebe. That I can promise you." He turned them back towards the house. "Let's get going. I'll make some calls and then we'll head out."

She stopped, her eyes on him, then reached up to kiss his cheek. "Thank you." She walked into the house ahead of him.

Andrew stood, hand on his cheek, a stunned look on his face, before moving after her. Yet, he turned to once more survey the backyard. Something was off there. Bill and the tech had found nothing, but Andrew knew they were being watched. How did he go back to work next week and leave her by herself?

* * * * *

Andrew turned to find his friend Jonah standing next to him, his eyes on Phoebe.

"I hear you two have quite the story." Jonah searched Andrew's face.

"We do, Jonah, and it's not over yet." Andrew turned to watch Phoebe as she laughed at Josiah and his wife, Faith. It had done her good, he thought. "Thanks for helping today."

"Not a problem, Andrew. Listen, I have to run. I've got to get ready for the workers to come in tomorrow." He paused. "Bring Phoebe out to the farm one day soon."

"I will, Jonah. Thank you." Andrew turned as Josiah approached.

"What next, Andrew? It looks as if we have the furniture out and the ladies are packing the last few boxes."

"I think we're about done then. I suggest we find somewhere to eat before we head back."

"I like that idea. Zeke and Paige are pushing for that."

"It looks as if our ladies are getting along well. I'm glad. Phoebe said she has no real friends."

Josiah stopped, turning back to Andrew. "Is that what she said? We'll have to fix that, now won't we?" He turned as he heard a commotion at the door.

"Phoebe! What is the meaning of this?"

Phoebe spun, her face going pale as she stared at the man standing there. She had hoped and prayed to be gone before he got word. "What are you doing here?"

"I came because the building manager called and told me my fiancée was moving out."

Andrew moved to stand behind Phoebe, his arms wrapping around her. Her hands came up to grasp his, her fingers white as she gripped his fingers hard.

"Not your fiancée, boy.  Never have been.  Never will be."

"Just what are you talking about?  Of course, you are.  Now, come on with me.  We'll talk this out.  You can have your hired men bring all your stuff back up to the apartment."

Josiah and Zeke had moved to flank Andrew.  Josiah could hear Faith speaking very quietly on the phone in the bedroom.

"Not happening.  So I suggest you leave."  Phoebe leaned back harder into Andrew.

The man stepped the room, his look disdainful as he looked at the three men.  He stared at Phoebe.

"Just what kind of game are you playing, Phoebe?  Of course we're engaged."

Andrew snorted, even as he eyed the three officers standing behind the man.

"Really?  Phoebe, you didn't tell me you were already engaged."  Andrew's voice held a tone to it his two friends recognized, one that meant he wasn't to be messed with.

She tilted her head to look back at him, catching the quick wink of his eye. Okay, so Andrew wanted to play. She'd play along.

"Guess I missed that one, didn't I? But I already have a husband, so why would I want a fiancée too?"

Ted's face grew red in his anger. "What do you mean, husband?"

Andrew finally had had enough and stepped around Phoebe.

"Phoebe has a husband and that would be me."

Ted stared at him and then with a quick movement, his fist landed on Andrew's jaw, knocking him off balance and to the floor. Ted was down and handcuffed before Phoebe had even reached Andrew.

Andrew sat up slowly, his hand to his jaw, before taking the hand Josiah reached down to help him up. Phoebe tucked herself under his arm, feeling safe close to him.

The first officer approached. "Lieutenant McBeth or is it Chief McBeth?"

Andrew gave a small tight smile. "Either one will do. I want charges pressed again him for assault, trespassing. He has a restraining order against him as well. His violation of that has to be included. And if you contact my detectives in Elmton, they'll have additional charges."

Ted stood, his eyes narrowed, as he listened. "Just what do you mean?"

The officer spun, his eyes hard as he responded. "This is a police officer that you struck. Charges will be filed against you. Even with your lawyer, you won't be out very soon." He nodded and Ted was led away. "I understand from our chief that you're still investigating Mrs. McBeth's kidnapping."

"Yes, we are. One of my detectives will be contacting yours in the next day or so to follow up." He reached to shake the officer's hand. "Thank you."

Phoebe watched him walk away, then turned to Andrew. "Your face?"

"It's nothing, Phoebe. I'm just glad Ted is put away."

She sighed as she looked over at the other two couples. "Unfortunately, it doesn't end it, does it? Thank you, Faith, for calling, and all of you. How can I really say thanks?"

"Not a problem, Phoebe. Now, are we done here?" Zeke looked around. "I would say about four more trips down and we're done."

"I'll find the manager, Phoebe. I want to have a word with him anyway. A little scare might do some good." Andrew watched as she hesitated and nodded. "Do you want to go with me?"

She shook her head. "No. I never felt comfortable around him either. You handle him."

Andrew knocked at the door of the manager's apartment and waited. He knew the man was in there. Finally, he hammered at the door.

"Open up. Police."

The man's head appeared in the crack of the door and he looked Andrew up and down.

"Whaddaya mean, police?"

Andrew pulled out his identification and shoved it into the man's face.

"Open up. I want to talk to you."

The man stepped back and Andrew moved forward until he stood just outside the open door.

"Phoebe Knight is now my wife. I understand you called Ted." The man stared at him, not giving an inch. Andrew sighed. "It's going to be like that, is it?" He saw the first responding officer heading back his way.

"Did you know there's a restraining order against him?  No?  So you willingly helped him violate it, did you?"  The man started to shake his head.  "Save it.  You know you did.  Officer, I think maybe you might want to speak with this gentleman.  And I would advise you obtain a search warrant."  Andrew nodded through the open door to the drugs laying on the table in the living room.

"Wait a minute.  You can't do that!"

The officer spoke.  "We can and we will.  Thanks, Chief McBeth.  We've been watching him but haven't been able to catch him until now."

Andrew watched as Phoebe and Paige talked, their heads close together.  Faith leaned in from the other side of Paige.  Andrew wasn't aware that both Zeke and Josiah had watched him over the day and now were exchanging glances, knowing how he felt. They nodded at each other.  Andrew had found his lady, even in the midst of danger, just like they did.

Andrew turned to Zeke.  "Zeke, we need to get our friends together for a meal, all of us."

Zeke nodded.  "Let me talk to Jonah and see if we can set up something at his place. With the farm, he has a lot more room than any of us do."

Josiah looked at his watch and then spoke. "Make it a potluck. I hate to break up the party, but I have to be on the road early in the morning to go see a client."

Zeke nodded. "Give me a call in the. morning, Andrew, when you're ready to unload the truck. Adam and Mark said they'd be available to help."

"Sounds good. Phoebe wants to donate the furniture to the furniture bank. She's also going to sort through her kitchen stuff, but most she says will go there as well."

Arm around Phoebe as they walked to the truck, Andrew scanned the area out of habit. Someone was out there, but he just couldn't see them. *Lord, see us safe. Help us to wrap this up quickly. Help me to court my wife as I should.*

Phoebe stood for a moment, looking up at him, before she climbed into the truck. *Why, Lord, why him? Is this what You planned for us so long ago?*

# Chapter 15

Phoebe rose from her knees, brushing off the dust from the garage floor. She looked around and sighed. Andrew was back at work today and she had decided to try sorting through her boxes. She seemed to be making more of a mess than accomplishing anything, and she knew why. She missed that oh-so-tall and handsome husband of hers. Not a day went by that he hadn't brought her flowers or done something nice for her. She smiled as she thought of the yellow roses he had walked in with on Saturday, a grin on his face, before he kissed her on the cheek. Her hand felt the spot.

Hearing the doorbell, she frowned. She wasn't expecting anyone, and Andrew had warned her to be very cautious when he wasn't around. Heading for the front door, she peeked out. Paige and Faith stood there as well as two other ladies. She opened the door, surprise on her face.

"Paige, Faith?  Come in.  I wasn't expecting you today."

Paige hugged her.  "We knew Andrew was back to work and you'd be lonely. We've come to help.  Andrew called me last night and told me he wanted us to help you paint, wallpaper, redecorate however you wanted."

"He did mention that, but it's his home."

Julia, Mark's wife, spoke up.  "No, it's your home, too, now, Phoebe, and Andrew wants you to make it yours.  I've known Andrew for years.  If he says you're to paint, then he means it."

"Oh, my!  Well, I guess then we paint. But I don't have any paint."

"What were you going when we came in?"  This from Matthias' Larkin.  "I'm Larkin by the way, married to Matthias.  We haven't met yet.  That's Julia, Mark's wife. Andrew's been friends with our husbands for years.  I know you met Jonah, he's not married, yet."  The four women laughed, and Larkin continued.  "Then, I know you met Adam the other day.  Samuel's been swamped or he would have been here.  Noah, Faith's cousin, travels a lot, but should be home soon, shouldn't he, Faith?"

"That's what he keeps telling Uncle Seth." Faith grinned, then turned to Phoebe. "OK, where do you want us to work?"

"I was out in the garage, trying to sort through boxes, but getting nowhere."

"Then, that's where we'll start." Faith headed for the kitchen. "I'll make the coffee and put on the kettle. We were in Riverville on Saturday and stopped at the Irish bakery there and picked up some goodies." She raised the box she held. "My treat for today."

* * * * *

Andrew sat behind his desk, staring at the paperwork in front of him. His eyes traced to the window across from his desk, a thoughtful look on his face. He had spoken to his captain with the county force the past Friday and had put in his resignation there. Being the police chief here was the right step, he knew, but he would miss the men and women of the county force.

He looked up at the tap on his door. Bill stood there. Andrew waved him in and to a chair.

Bill entered, shutting the door behind him, his eyes on his friend and chief.

"How're you doing, Andrew?"

Andrew shrugged. "I didn't want to leave Phoebe on her own today, I can tell you that much. And coming back to all this paperwork!"

Bill laughed. "I'm glad to turn it over to you. Believe it or not, it was all caught up Friday night when I left. I made sure of that."

"I appreciate that." Andrew leaned back in his chair. "Bring me up to speed on the investigations."

Two hours later, Bill stood. "Coffee, Andrew? I'm ready for one."

"Not yet. I have some calls to return. Thanks, Bill. You've done a good job."

"Andrew? Did you decide which hat you're going to wear?"

Andrew looked up at Bill's keen eyes and nodded. "I have. The word will be out officially later today. I'm here for the long haul. Now that I'm married and hopefully someday a father, I don't want to be out on the road like I was. This feels better. I have peace about it."

"Good. Just so you know, I've asked for the lead detective spot here now that Foxcroft has retired."

"Glad to hear."

Late that afternoon, Andrew opened his front door and stopped, delicious odours meeting his nose.  It was like walking into home, he thought, trying to decide what all he was smelling.  He walked to the kitchen, a smile on his face.  Phoebe turned from the counter, her face lighting up as she saw him, before crossing the room for his hug.

"I'm so glad you're home, Andrew."

"Me, too.  Something smells good."

"Just a roast and an apple pie."

Andrew sighed.  "You've picked my favourite foods, you know."  He leaned back so he could see her face.  "Have a good day?"

"I did.   Your four friends' wives dropped by this morning and helped me sort through the boxes.  Then we headed out to the local hardware store and picked up some paint chips."  She searched his face.  "Are you sure, Andrew?"

"Sure?  About what?  That you can redecorate, paint, whatever?  Of course, I am.  My house is kind of boring.  Mom's been after me for years to do something with it.  I had no motivation until now.  Make it your own, love.  It's your home too."  He dropped a kiss on her forehead.  "Now, do I have time to shower and clean up before dinner?"

"You do." She waited for him to let her go. When he didn't, she gave him a searching look. "You have to let me go, you know."

He tightened his hug. "I know I do, but I kind of like what I'm holding right now."

With a laugh, she shoved him towards the hallway. "Go on. Get yourself cleaned up. I'll have supper on in about twenty minutes."

Andrew watched her for a minute, then headed for the bedroom. He sure liked coming home to Phoebe there. He wondered how in such a short time, she had become such a huge part of his day and life.

Later that evening, Phoebe turned as Andrew approached her, his arm coming around her and leading her outside to the glider. She snuggled against him, peace once more flowing over her.

"Phoebe, I talked to Bill today. They're still moving ahead with the investigation but it's far from over. Ted isn't talking. Nor is your family." He sighed, a distressed look on his face. "The more he digs, the deeper they are in whatever was going on."

"How did I not know, Andrew? How was I so blind?"

"God was protecting you, I think, love. Sometimes He gives us blindness or deafness just to protect us." He stared into the distance as he pushed his foot into the wooden deck to get the glider working. "I'm just so thankful He chose me to help you."

"Me, too." She was silent for a while. "I've tried to think of anyone else I might know who would be involved, but I just don't know. Do you think they have accounts overseas?"

Andrew nodded. "We have a forensics accountant looking at that possibility. He's good, so if there's anything there, he'll find it."

"But what do we do in the meantime? I can't stay hidden in the house all the time."

"I know, and that worries me."

Phoebe was quiet for a while, then spoke. "I have a bunch of boxes to get rid of, Andrew, ready to donate. There's also some garbage."

"Not a problem, love. We'll get rid of them. I can load them up on the truck and drop them off tomorrow, if you like."

"Thank you." She nestled closer, her love for Andrew growing minute by minute.

She didn't really know how he felt though and would never ask.

Andrew looked around in the darkness, wondering what felt off. He knew something was, but still he couldn't put his finger on it. Tomorrow night, he would tear the yard apart if necessary to find out what it was.

"Do you have plans for tomorrow?" Andrew's voice was quiet, not wanting to disturb the peace he sensed in Phoebe.

She shrugged. "Your Mom called. She wants to pick me up for lunch. Is it safe?"

"It should be. Mom knows how to handle herself. I've seen her put Dad down. And she's put me down in the last couple of years."

"Really? I'll have to take lessons from her."

Andrew laughed. "That would be a good idea."

## *Chapter 16*

$\mathscr{P}$hoebe watched as Emily sat down across the table from her at the small diner she had insisted they needed to eat at. Emily had shown up early that morning and swept Phoebe out with her, taking her to home furnishings stores.

"I still don't see what's wrong with Andrew's furniture." Phoebe was genuinely puzzled.

"It's men's furniture, my dear. Not couple's furniture. We needed to find you couple's furniture."

Phoebe started to laugh at that. "Actually, I like Andrew's furniture."

Emily sat back, a look of pretend horror on her face. "Please, don't say that. You need new furniture."

Phoebe shook her head, a grin in place. "No, we don't, not really. I mean I wouldn't mind an easy chair for me, but other than that,

I'm fine with what he has. You should have seen my furniture."

Emily began to laugh. "I did. Drew sent me pictures."

"He didn't really, did he?"

Emily looked up as she heard her name called, then rose to hug the woman who had approached. "Ev! I was hoping you'd be here today."

"Aren't I here every day?" She turned to Phoebe. "And who is this?"

"This is Drew's Phoebe, Ev. Phoebe, this is my sister, Evalina. We call her Ev."

Ev took a look at Phoebe, then swept her into a huge hug. "I always wondered what Drew's lady would be like. You're a keeper."

Phoebe sat, mouth open, not quite sure what she had heard, as Emily started laughing.

"Stop, Ev. You'll have her running for the hills before we even have lunch."

Ev laughed and then hugged Phoebe again. "Welcome to the family, Phoebe. We're a little be fun loving. Can you tell?"

Phoebe smiled, still not sure. Her eyes drifted past the two woman to the window and her heart sank. There was that man again, the one who had been watching her weeks ago. Now what?

Emily had been watching her face and saw the change. "Phoebe? Is everything all right?"

Phoebe shook her head. "No. That man is back and outside watching us."

Ev turned as if to go to the kitchen and studied him. "He's been hanging around here the last few days. I'll take care of him." She walked away to the kitchen.

"Emily, what's she going to do?" Phoebe was scared.

"Let her handle it. Her son is a federal agent or officer or something like that. He helps in the kitchen when he's around and Avery must be here today. Yep, he is. He just took your stalker away."

Phoebe's eyes flew to the window. "Great, but he can't be the only one."

"He not likely is. Let's eat, then I want to look at Drew's garden. I doubt he's done much with it lately."

"He hasn't, but I have. I've had time on my hands and needed something to do."

Emily eyed Phoebe. "Time on your hands, have you? Then I have work for you.

Our regular secretary is out on sick leave and we've been trying to manger without her. We're not even sure if she'll be coming back. How would you like to work for Simon and me?"

Phoebe's eyes lit up. "I would love to, but I should talk to Andrew first."

Emily shook her head. "He's the one who suggested you. He knows how hard it is for you to be sitting still. So? Want to work for some PIs?"

Phoebe started to laugh, Emily delighted with how her face lit up. Drew, if she doesn't have your heart by now, you're blind.

* * * * *

Andrew walked into his home late that afternoon, not hearing Phoebe. Concerned, he searched for her. She had to be here somewhere, he thought, for the alarm to be off. Opening the back door, he stepped outside and saw her, kneeling at the garden at the back, hands deep into the dirt. He paced towards her, watching as she stilled and then turned, a smile lighting up her face.

"You're home, Andrew!"

"I am. And you're dirty." He grinned at the frown she threw his way.

"I know. I meant to have this done and be cleaned up before you got home. What time is it?"

"It's okay. We don't have to eat on any particular schedule." He dropped down to sit beside her. "Tell me, are you just playing in the dirt or do you have a reason for digging here?"

"Your mother insisted we needed more plants today and took me to a garden centre. I've just finished with the last of them." She sat back, using her forearm to brush back her hair. "I have fun today. You're so fortunate to have a mother like that." She was pensive, and Andrew tilted his head to watch her. "She took me to lunch at your Auntie Ev's." Phoebe looked up, fear crossing her face for a moment. "That man was there, but your cousin took care of him."

"Avery?" At her nod, Andrew stared into the distance before studying her face. "He dropped by my office. He had quite a story to tell me. I can't give you all the details, but the federal authorities are looking into your parents as well."

Phoebe's face paled, and then she nodded. "That doesn't surprise me." She turned, her eyes searching the yard. "Andrew, over there. I found something that

I don't think is part of your solar lights. Will you take a look at it, please?"

Andrew reached for the solar light Phoebe had pointed to and he knew then what had seemed off to him in the yard.

"This isn't a regular solar light, Phoebe."

"It's not?"

He shook his head. "I'm betting there's a camera inside or a listening device, if not both." He stared at it for a moment, then replaced it. "We'll leave it here for now. Come on, love. Let's get you cleaned up. I'm taking my sweetheart out for dinner tonight."

She stopped, her abrupt movement stopping him. "Andrew?"

"Yes, love?" He turned to watch her face.

"Am I really that? Your sweetheart?"

He nodded, seeing the softening of her face. "You are, love, and have been since the first moment I saw you in that roadhouse."

"Thank you, Drew. I needed to hear that." She moved into his space and his hug. "Now what?"

He grinned. "First, I take my lady to dinner and then we cuddle on the couch?"

She smacked him. "That's not what I meant."

"It wasn't? Then maybe this is." He bent, his lips finding hers, both of them tightening arms around one another.

The man watching cursed, knowing it would be more difficult to get to her now.

✳ ✳ ✳ ✳ ✳

Andrew watched the next morning through the glass into the interrogation room. Ted was there, with his lawyer, and Bill and Lily had just entered. He wondered if this would be the day he finally talked. He snorted. Not likely, he thought.

Finally, Bill left, leaving Lily with the two. He found Andrew and shook his head.

"He's not talking, Andrew. I have no idea what we can say that will make him talk."

Andrew ran his hand through his hair. "I have no idea either." Then he stopped, his eyes turning to Bill. "Would you be a betting man, Bill?"

"Not really. Why?"

"I suspect that apartment manager and Bill had a nice little game going with the drugs. Try that angle and see what you come up with. That manager called him to come when Phoebe was there, and he wouldn't have done it just for money, I don't think."

"Good thought. I'll see what I can do with that."

Andrew walked away, knowing Bill would do his best to find the information they needed. It was almost time to leave for home, but something was prodding him. He stood in his office, wondering what it was that had caught at his memories.

Then, he sat, knowing what it was. He pulled up one of the databases he used and searched. There is was, he thought. There's the connection. But how do we prove it?

He looked up as Bill stood as his doorway.

"How'd it go?"

Bill entered, slumping into a chair. "He refuses to talk. Even with the evidence we have against him, he hasn't said a word. I talked to the psychologist. He thinks Ted's so scared, he can't and won't say anything about who his cronies are."

"That makes sense. I found something, Bill, that I need you to follow up on." Andrew pointed at his printer. "Take that and work on it. But first, go home. Don't come back until Monday. You need a break and will work better for it."

Bill nodded as he studied the paperwork. "How'd you make this connection?"

"Just something Avery said this morning, about Phoebe's parents and sisters. Somehow, there's a huge connection out there we haven't found yet. And I think it comes back to someone here in our town."

Bill nodded once more as he looked up. "I suspect you're right. You heading out soon?"

Andrew looked down at his desk, knowing his paperwork was done. "I am. I'm glad it's Friday, Bill. I just wish we could find the connection and end this. I have a bad feeling in my gut that something's about to break loose."

"I know that feeling, Andrew. Go home."

# Chapter 17

Silas watched as Andrew and Phoebe walked towards him before church on Sunday morning. He nodded, knowing that he had been right about the two of them. Lord, You knew. You prepared this two for one another. Now what, though? How do we get them through the next while, keeping them safe from harm?

"Andrew. Phoebe. It's good to see you two here."

Andrew stopped, his eyes on Silas. "How did you know, Silas?"

"Know what?"

Andrew shook his head. "You know what I mean. You've done this before with others."

Silas smiled even as he shrugged. "It's the Lord, Andrew. I'm just His tool."

Phoebe looked between the two men, puzzled. Then, her face cleared. "Matchmaker, are you, Silas?"

Silas stared at her, then started to laugh. "I guess I am, Phoebe. And how are you this fine day?"

"I'm good, Silas. And thank you." Her quiet words only reached to the two men beside her.

Silas nodded. "You're welcome. Listen, I know you two likely have plans, but can you come for lunch today? I'd be glad to have you."

Andrew stared down at Phoebe for a moment, then nodded. "We can. We'll see you after church."

Silas watched the congregation as they sat from the last song before the message. His message today would rock them to the core, he knew. *Lord, I sure hope You know what You're doing, because I sure don't.*

"Today, it's just another day for some, isn't it?" Silas looked out over the sanctuary, searching for those he knew were hurting. "I could give you platitudes and easy words, but that's not me. You know me.

"In Jeremiah 18, the prophet talks about watching a potter work on a clay pot. When something went wrong, he shaped another pot. He made something beautiful out of something damaged.

"Isaiah clearly states that we are the clay, God is our Potter. We are clay shaped by His hands. He knows our weaknesses, our frailties, our strengths. He wants to shape us to serve Him. How many of us let Him do just that? Being human and having a free will, it's tough to take hands off our lives and let Him do what He must and can to shape us to who He wants us to be. I must admit, I struggle some days just to do that. Be open to Him, my friends. Let Him have your lives. He makes beautiful pottery out of our lives."

Phoebe sat, lost in thought as the last hymn played and through the last prayer. Andrew sat, his arm along the back of the pew, just waiting and watching her.

She finally turned, catching his eyes. "Silas is right, isn't he? That's what your Mom does when something happens to one of the pots she's working on, doesn't she?" At his nod, she sat back, her eyes on the front of the church. "Now, it makes sense, Andrew, what I'm going through. He's shaping me to what He wants."

Andrew's arm dropped to her shoulders as he drew her close. "Some people never get it, do they, love? You have. Come on. Let's go find our pastor and have lunch."

* * * * *

Andrew was deep in paperwork Wednesday morning when one of the patrol officers appeared at his door.

"We have a bomb threat, Chief."

Andrew stood, heading for the door. "Where?"

"The library, of all places. We've evacuated and our bomb squad is getting ready to move in."

Andrew stood a few minutes later near the fire chief's truck, watching as the bomb squad moved in.

"Andrew?" He turned as Bill approached. "What more do we know?"

Andrew shrugged. "Not a lot. It's strange they would target the library though."

"Where's Phoebe?"

Andrew spun at his question. "It's Wednesday?" His eyes slid closed. "She was to have been here today." He searched the crowds, not seeing her.

"Call her. I'll grab a couple of patrol officers and see if she's here."

Andrew listened at Phoebe's phone went to voice mail. Where are you, love? Not here, I hope. He turned as he heard his name called.  Bill walked towards, a grim look on his face.

"Bill?"

"I found her, Andrew.  She's safe.  I've tucked her away with Lily and Jason."  He held out a letter.  "She had this in her hands."

"What?"  Andrew stared down at the envelope.  "She hasn't opened it yet."

"No.  She says she found it just as the call came in.  What kind of games are they playing?  And you know how the press works.  They'll somehow blame her for this."

Andrew sighed.  "I know.  We need to get our PR guys working on this."  He turned the envelope over and over.  "Find one of our techs and open this with them."

Bill nodded, then turned, searching the crowd.  Finding who he wanted, he walked away, his thoughts racing.  Who had done this now, he wondered?

The tech listened as Bill spoke, then took the envelope, dusting for prints and then opening it.  Her eyes flew to Bill's as they read the note.  Bill turned to search for Andrew and then Phoebe.  Things had just changed.  Neither were safe.  Andrew would not back down, he knew, not even if it meant his life.  Phoebe, he could pretty much assume that she wouldn't either.

"Run your magic on that, please?  I need to find the chief.  First, let me take a photo of that so I can show him."

Andrew turned from speaking with the bomb squad leader.  A hoax, he thought, but why?  What was the purpose?

Bill appeared at his side, handing him his phone in silence.  Andrew's face hardened as he read.

"I would say they're getting desperate, aren't they?"

"They are, Andrew.  They've made you a target now as well as Phoebe."

Andrew rubbed the back of his neck, feeling eyes on him.  "I am, but I can't walk away from any of you.  We need to track this guy down and fast."

"We've been trying, Andrew.  Phoebe's told us everything she can.  She's even gone back through any paperwork she has.  She doesn't know anything else."  He turned, watching as the teams packed up to leave.  "She also says she hasn't talked to her parents or sisters since you were there."

"No, she hasn't.  She hasn't wanted to.  They certainly didn't care if she was there or not." Andrew's voice died away. "Bill, can you run something for me? Phoebe doesn't look like her parents and certainly not her sisters. Can you try and find out if she was adopted or something like that? Any missing children that would have fit her description from when she was a baby or toddler?"

Bill stared at Phoebe, then back at Andrew. "You don't think?"

"I may be grasping at straws, Bill, but we need to check this out. Just a feeling I have."

"I know your feelings too well, Andrew, and they're usually bang on. It would explain a lot. I'll make sure Phoebe gets home safely. You should go talk to her."

Andrew laughed. "That's where I'm heading. Have someone run her car home. I'm bringing her in with me. We need to have a meeting again, just to go over things with her. She's getting anxious, not knowing what's going on."

"And so's her husband." Bill laughed as Andrew spun to stare at him.

Phoebe turned as she heard her name called and was swept into Andrew's arms. She clung to him, her shudders finally easing.

"You okay, love?" Andrew's quiet words whispered to her heart.

She nodded. "I am now. What happened, Andrew?"

"We're working on it, love, but first, your keys. I'm having an officer drop your car off at home." He stilled and turned, Phoebe still in his arms. "Bill!"

Bill turned at Andrew's call and ran towards him. "What did you want, Andrew?"

"We checked the library, but not the vehicles."

Bill's face showed shock, then hardened. "Tom's still here. Let me get him. Keys?"

Phoebe handed over her keys, even as she watched Andrew's face. "Andrew?"

"We need to check your car, Phoebe. Then I'll have someone drive it home for you. I want you to come with me."

She nodded, even as she watched the bomb squad leader suit up again before heading towards her car.

Late that afternoon, Andrew looked up from his paperwork, his eyes on Phoebe as she sat on the couch, her eyes on her book. He hadn't heard yet from the bomb squad and that worried him. He rose and walked to the door, looking down the hallway and seeing Tom headed his way.

"Tom?" Andrew met him halfway down the hallway.

"You were right on with that, Andrew. There was a bomb. Very tricky to defuse too. Someone knows what they're doing."

Andrew slumped against the wall. "I was praying there wouldn't be one. This changes everything."

Tom nodded as he watched Andrew. "It does. This one would have gone off as soon as she hit the key fob. She wouldn't have survived, Andrew. Nor would anyone in a fifty-yard circumference."

Andrew's face whitened. "I guess we know now what they're planning." His eyes went to his office doorway. "Somehow, I have to keep her safe and alive."

Tom nodded. "I'll have my report on your desk in the morning. Just so you know, all of us have been talking. Your officers are planning to help on their time off. They're setting up a schedule now of who can be with Phoebe at any time you're not."

Andrew nodded. "Thank them for me, Tom. I need to go find my wife and then, I don't know what."

"We'll find them, Andrew. Trust me on that. We'll find them and get them to justice, keeping you both safe at the same time."

Andrew nodded once again. "I guess I have a guard now too, don't I?"

Tom stood for a moment, his eyes thoughtful. "You do. If they can't get to Phoebe, then they'll try and use you. I would suggest you not put yourself out there too much."

"I can't hide behind my desk, Tom. You know that. Thanks again."

Andrew stood for a moment watching Phoebe before he dropped to the couch beside her, a sigh finding its way out.

"Andrew?"

Andrew looked at her and then pulled her close. "There was a bomb in your car, love. It would have killed you."

Phoebe shuddered, a blankness coming over her. "Why?"

"That's what we're working on, love. Tom from the bomb squad just left. He told me that the officers are making up a schedule so someone can be with you at all times, when I'm not."

She shrugged. "Is that what you want?" At his nod, she continued. "Then, that's the way it will be. The press is going to have a heyday with this, you know."

"I know. I have our PR people working on a statement." He hesitated, not quite sure how to ask the next question. "Phoebe, have you ever had reason to doubt your parents were really your parents?"

She tilted her head to watch him, her eyes studying his face. "You know, as I grew up, more and more I wondered that. I don't look like any of them. Hair colour, eyes, build - nothing matches them or my grandparents or aunts and uncles. Do you have a reason for asking?"

He sighed. "Just a suspicion I have, love. I've asked Bill to search through your history and to see if there are any reports of missing children who would be about your age."

She nodded. "Let's get your parents working on this, if they have time. If we can find something, then we can petition the courts to open the records. Or I can register to find my birth parents. That's being done now, but it can be a long process."

"That it is. I can feel you thinking, love. What are you plotting?"

She looked up at him in protest, seeing the mischief and love shining in his eyes. "I'm thinking that I register anyway on one of the adoption finder sites."

"You could do that."

"I don't get it, though, Andrew. How would that fit with what's happening?"

"I'm not sure yet, love. I'm still trying to reason it through." He looked away from her for a moment and then back. "We'll figure it out. Right now, let's get you home."

"But you're not finished here."

"I am for the night. I'll pick it back up tomorrow.

# Chapter 18

*T*urning as she heard her name called, Phoebe waited for Faith to catch up with her.

"Phoebe, this is so nice. I was hoping to see you soon." She reached out to hug her friend.

"It is nice, Faith. Do you have time for a coffee? I've been shopping and just need a break?"

"I do." Faith's brow wrinkled as Phoebe turned to the man standing beside her and spoke. "What's going on, Phoebe? It looks as if you have a guard."

Phoebe sighed. "I do. I have had for the last couple of days. Thank goodness, it's Friday and Andrew will be home for the weekend."

Faith waited until they had given their orders and then spoke. "A guard? That doesn't sound good."

"It's not. I can't go into details, but the force has decided that Andrew and I need to be watched all the time.  I feel like I live in a fish bowl."  She looked up as she heard her name.

"Phoebe!  So glad you came again."  Ev reached to hug her.

"Auntie Ev!  I've been trying to get it but it's been hard.  This is Faith, a friend. Faith, this is Andrew's Auntie Ev."

They chatted for a few minutes before Ev moved on.  Phoebe watched as each patron came and went.

Finally, Faith spoke.  "Is there a time or day that would work for both you and Andrew to come to dinner? Uncle Seth wants to meet you."

"Your uncle?"

"He does.  He really likes and respects your husband and wants to meet the woman, and I quote, who stole his heart."  Faith laughed at the expression on Phoebe's face, then sobered.  "Have they found the men yet?"

Phoebe shook her head, her eyes on the officer sitting near her.  "No, they haven't, not that Andrew's said."  She sighed.  "He also thinks that maybe I was adopted or something and that plays into it."

Faith sat back, her eyes on her friend. "But why? And how?"

Phoebe shrugged. "Maybe because I don't look like any of them? I just don't get it, Faith. Who does this to their own children?"

Faith nodded. "I know, Phoebe. Let's you and I do some digging."

"I can't ask that of you. It's too dangerous."

Faith started to laugh. "Honey, you ain't seen nothing. Josiah and I went through our own trials and danger. We actually eloped."

"You didn't!" Phoebe stared at her friend, then started to laugh. "Well, then, that makes two couples that did, doesn't it?" She slid from her chair and reached to hug Faith. "Thank you, Faith. I needed this today. And I'll talk to Andrew about a date for a meal. Let me cook this time. And your little one's fine in our home."

"I would like that. I hear Emily took you furniture shopping."

Phoebe laughed as she headed out of the diner. "She did. She was shocked when I refused to give up most of Andrew's stuff."

"I'm sure she was."

Phoebe stood and watched her walk away, before turning to the officer. "I think I'd like to head home, if you don't mind."

"Not a problem. Let's get you away from here." His eyes searched the area, feeling like they were being watched.

* * * * *

It was late when Andrew walked wearily away from his car, stopping to speak to the officer waiting outside. He unlocked the door, not surprised to see the house in darkness. Tucking his shoes into the closet, he dropped his briefcase on his desk, then unloaded his weapon and stashed both weapon and ammunition into the safe. He stretched, glad the week was over and it was Friday night. Tonight's meeting with the mayor had gone well, he thought, but he wished he could do these meeting during the day. He headed for the kitchen, not hungry, but needing water.

He stopped at Phoebe's bedroom, the door open. She wasn't there. He spun, not quite sure where she would be. Seeing a low light coming from his bedroom, he paced that way, anxiety growing that fled as he reached the door. He smiled. Phoebe was curled up in his bed, sound asleep. He quietly changed and then slid into bed, his arms reaching for his wife and snuggling her to his chest. Weary to the bone, his eyes slid closed and he slept.

Phoebe awakened the next morning, disoriented for a moment, then turned to search the room. Andrew was still asleep and she took a moment to study him before she slid from the bed and headed for her room to change. She needed to talk to him and soon, about what she had discovered. She had waited for him to come home last night but sleep had overtaken her.

She wondered what he would say about her findings. She sighed. She already knew what he would say. It was just what they had expected, she thought. She hadn't thought that she would get an answer so quickly.

Andrew stood for a moment, watching Phoebe work away at breakfast before moving into her space to pour himself a coffee. She turned to greet him, stopping at the look on his face.

"Andrew?"

"Phoebe, we need to talk."

She nodded. "Before we talk about what you want to talk about, I need to tell you something. Here." She handed him a plate of waffles before seating herself and reaching for his hand as he said grace. She waited for him to start eating, then spoke. "I did some research, Andrew. You were right. I was adopted."

Andrew's hands rested on the table, his fork and knife forgotten. "You did some research."

"I did. I joined one of those adoption websites that help connect families. I found mine." She looked up, tears on her face. "They never gave me up willingly, Andrew. It says I was stolen as a six-month-old. Why?"

"Ah, Phoebe." Andrew was on his knees beside her, wrapping her in his arms. "We'll find out, love. We'll find out."

She nodded against his chest. "I sent Bill the information. He said he would talk to you."

"I hadn't seen him yesterday morning. I was in meetings all day." He leaned back. "I think we need to get away for a couple of days."

She stared at him. "How can we?"

"Leave it to me. Jonah wanted us to come to the farm, but I think the cabin would be better. We need to talk over a lot of things, and not just this."

She sighed, knowing he was right. "We do, Andrew."

He sat back on his chair to finish his breakfast. "How be we leave right after we finish? Just pack up some of our food and drinks and we can go." He watched as she mentally went through the food they would need to take. "And Phoebe?" He waited until she looked at him. "I liked finding you where you were last night."

She blushed. "I was waiting up for you and went to sleep."

"I figured as much."

* * * * *

Andrew turned from watching the road behind them. He thought they had reached the cabin without being followed but nowadays, he just wasn't sure. He knew Phoebe was out behind the cabin, looking for what, he had no idea. He headed that way, stopping as he watched her kneeling in front of the perennial bed his Mom had planted, her hands deep into the dirt.

"Phoebe?"

She looked up as he approached, face alight. "Yes, Andrew?"

"How come I always catch you playing in the dirt?"

She started to laugh as she sat back on the ground. "I have no idea. I love the feel of dirt between my fingers. I was never allowed to garden, but I used to sneak out and help our gardener. He always had time for me and I was alone a lot."

Andrew's head tilted. "That bothered you, didn't it?"

She nodded, her face pensive. "I always felt like I didn't fit in, didn't belong to them. I always tried, too hard I guess. But now that I know I wasn't really theirs, it makes sense. Did you talk to Bill?"

He shook his head. "Bill would have called if he had something. And he hadn't before we left. I sent him a text that we'd be away until tomorrow night."

"Your family's not coming up, are they?"

"No. The girls are away with their families, and Mom and Dad are in the middle of an investigation they can't leave. So the cabin would have been sitting empty if we hadn't come."

"Are we safe?"

He searched the area with his eyes before looking at her. "I would like to say definitely that we are, but I can't. Somehow they keep finding you and I don't know how. We've gone over all the officers and department staff. Not one would give your location away."

"So, someone has to be watching us. Would your Dad know if they had hired an investigator?"

"Good question. He might. I'll call him tomorrow night and ask."

Phoebe leaned back on her hands, her face tilted to the sun. "This is nice, Andrew. I wish we could live here year round." She brought her eyes back to him. "Can you tell me where the investigation stands?"

He sighed, knowing they needed to talk, but not wanting to break into the peace of the day. "I can tell you what I'm able to. Ted still hasn't talked. We're still looking at your parents and sisters. The forensics accountant has found accounts overseas in their names, but he's still working through it. Dr. Ledley has been arrested and faces charges of dealing prescription painkillers." He sighed. "There's just so much we need to find out to tie it all together. "

"I know. You'll get there." She rose and waited for him. "It's lunchtime. Can we pack a picnic and head out somewhere to eat?"

"We can, love.  There's a rock not far from here that Mom used to call our picnic table.  It's big and flat."

That evening, Andrew stood, arm on the rough wood mantle, and stared down at the empty fireplace.  His thoughts were all over the place, and that wasn't like him.  He was usually organized.  He sighed, knowing that the situation with Phoebe had changed him, had made him fearful, had made him want to pack up and run.

He turned as he hear soft footsteps coming towards him and smiled.  Phoebe had long ago pulled off her socks and shoes and was padding around barefoot, enjoying the freedom to do so.  She had told him that she was never allowed to do that, never allowed to walk around in her sock feet.

"Andrew, here.  You left your coffee."

"Thanks, love."  He took it from her and studied her face.  "You seem more at peace today."

"I am, Andrew.  Yesterday, I was in shock, then scared.  Today, I understand that God has a plan.  That's what I'm not sure of.  I do know now that it includes you."

He set his mug down on the mantle and reached for her.  "I was praying you'd say that.  I can't imagine my life without you in it now." He stared down at her. "We need to work through where we want to go. I want to court you, as Dad says, for the rest of your life. But first, we need to find out who's after you and why."

"That's the elephant in the room, isn't it?" She moved to throw herself down on the couch, head on the back so she could stare at the ceiling. "How close are you to finding it all out?"

Andrew shrugged. "I have no idea, Phoebe. I've been keeping hands off, just so nothing could be said. Bill gives me an update as he needs to." He sat beside her, reaching for her hand. "We're praying our way through it, Phoebe, as are our friends."

"I know. I'm just impatient I guess. I've been dealing with this for too many years."

"What do you mean?"

She turned her head so she could stare at him. "I never told you, did I?" When he shook his head, she continued, "I've always felt something off about the money they made. I tried to get information on it one day but they came home before I found out it all." She sat up. "Dummy me. I took photos of what I had found and stuck them in a safety deposit box in a bank here in Elmton. I didn't want word getting back to them that I had a safety deposit box. I think they have a lot of bankers on their payroll or who owe them favours."

"Do you realize, Phoebe, that you've just opened up a new avenue of investigation?"

She sighed, then mischief sparkled in her eyes. "How much will Bill hate me on that one?"

Andrew started laughing. "Not too much, I hope, but I think we were already heading that way with the banks. Any names would be helpful."

She snorted and Andrew stared at her. "Try any bank in that town and surrounding towns. Think bank managers, upper staff, investment staff." Her voice slowed. "That's what's been bugging me. Try the investment staff at First Bank."

"You're sure?"

"I'm sure. They were too close to some of them, and conversations I overheard didn't fit with just regular investments."

Andrew nodded. "Then, I'll tell Bill on Monday. Right now, though, I think I would just like to snuggle with my wife for a while."

"You would, would you?" She smiled, an imp of mischief sparkling out again. "And does your wife want to do that too?"

"I hope she does.  Hey wait! Come back here!"  Andrew was on his feet and running after Phoebe as she dashed for the back door. "Where are you heading?"

She stopped near the glider.  "Right here.  We can snuggle and glide out here and enjoy the stars overhead."

# Chapter 19

*M*onday morning found Andrew searching the department for Bill without success. He finally tracked down Lily.

"Lily, do you know where Bill is?"

Lily looked up and smiled. "Andrew! Hi! No, I'm sorry. He found out something on Friday afternoon and said he'd be late getting in today as he had to travel to Oak City this morning."

"Didn't say what, did he?"

She shook her head. "No, he didn't. Can I help?"

Andrew looked down at the papers he was holding and then at Lily. "How deep into the investigation are you about Phoebe?"

"Way too deep, Andrew. Every time we think we're getting to the end, something or someone else turns up. Why?"

Andrew sighed as he held out the papers. "Then, this should fit right in. Phoebe did some research on her own last week. This is what she found. Keep it between you and Bill, please? And if you could give my Dad a call, he said he had information he wanted to pass on as well."

"I can do that." She studied him, seeing the lines stress was putting on his face. "Did you get any rest this weekend?"

"I did, thanks for asking. We headed to the cabin on Saturday morning. It was nice and quiet up there."

He turned as he heard footsteps. Bill stood there, a frown on his face.

"Andrew?'

"Bill. I just dropped off some material for you two. Do you need to talk?"

Bill shook his head, an unreadable look crossing his face. "Not right now. I'll catch up with you this afternoon. Is Phoebe okay?"

"She is for now. Is there a reason for asking?"

Bill sighed, then shook his head. "Nothing I can pin down. Sources are still talking that there are contracts out on both of you. Why you, I have no idea."

"That's nice to know. If you find out, let me know." Bill watched Andrew walk away, then turned to Lily.

"Lily?"

She nodded. "Phoebe was right on. She's not a biological member of that family. I'll need to do more searching, but she thinks she was abducted when she was just months old."

Bill sank into his chair, his face thoughtful. "That makes sense in a bizarre way, but why?"

Jason Long, another detective, stuck his head into the office. "And I think I know why." He quickly brought the two sitting there up to date on what he had found. "We need to alert Andrew."

Bill nodded. "We do. Let's find out what we can this morning. I'll talk to him this afternoon."

＊ ＊ ＊ ＊ ＊

Phoebe turned as she heard the doorbell ring. She peeked out, her face whitening. There was no way she was answering the door. Her parents stood there. How had they found her? She hadn't given them her address and she knew Andrew hadn't. There was no way they could have found out.

She turned, looking for her phone, as the female officer approached her and pointed at the door. Phoebe drew her back into the office.

"It's my parents, and I don't want to see them. How did they find us anyway?"

The office nodded, then spoke into her phone, drawing Phoebe back into the corner of the room where she couldn't be seen.

"There are officers on the way. They'll be discreet but will get them away. There's nothing to show that you're home, is there?"

Phoebe shook her head as the doorbell rang again, shudders running through her body. "There isn't. You don't have a car parked out front, and mine is in the garage." She looked up in horror. "If they go to the back door, I can't remember locking it."

"I did as I headed through to find you. Now, let's be quiet."

They waited for what seemed an eternity before the officer's phone buzzed. She looked at it quickly and then nodded to Phoebe.

"They're gone. They were gone by the time the officers arrived. We'll stay here until they sweep the area around the house."

"You don't think...." Phoebe's voice died away at the possibilities.

"We don't but we don't take any chances. We like Andrew too much to let anything happen to his wife. He's the best chief any of us have served under."

Phoebe turned as she heard keys in the front door and then Andrew's voice. She flew from the office into his arms, finding refuge there. Andrew looked up at the officer and nodded.

"Thank you, Penny."

"Not a problem, Andrew. I'll just check with the officers outside."

"Phoebe, talk to me." Andrew felt the shudders easing.

"Why did they come, Andrew? And how did they find your address?"

"That's a good question, Phoebe. Listen, I think we're going to have to go somewhere else for a few days. I know. You don't want to. Neither do I. It's that, or I take you to work with me every day and set you up somewhere to work."

"I like that option but it would be distracting for you."

"No, it wouldn't. I've been told by the mayor and the council to do what I need to do to keep you safe. Without you knowing it, they've seen you and some have met you at church. You have quite a following, love."

"I do? I don't like that."

Andrew gave a small laugh, then stood back, hands on her upper arms. "We have to do something. Your parents finding us shows they're desperate."

"I know. I can't figure out how they knew."

Andrew turned as Bill tapped at the door and then entered.

"Bill?"

"We found them sitting in the car down the street a block. We've taken them in for questioning. We have enough evidence right now to charge them for extortion and fraud as well as money laundering. We're working through other charges." He turned to Phoebe. "That doesn't mean you're safe. If they found you, then others can find you."

"I know." She leaned back against Andrew. "But where do we go? Andrew has to be in the office every day."

"Actually, I can work from just about anywhere, but I do need to be there for some days. Bill, can you find us somewhere we can be safe?"

He nodded. "I can. Richard has agreed to help." Richard had a security team and stepped in as needed. "He'll have a place for you two. He'll also be able to help get you back and forth to the office. He suggests on the days you need to be there that Phoebe be there as well."

Both nodded before Andrew spoke. "That's how we'll play it then. Let's go pack some stuff, Phoebe. We'll try and find something to amuse you."

She smacked his arm as she turned. "Amuse me? Get a life, Andrew. I have things I want to do. Research. College courses to pursue."

"Wait a minute, Phoebe. You can't take your laptop."

She spun to stare at Bill. "And why not?"

"Richard won't let you. But he'll have one you can use."

She sighed. "Life sucks, you know."

Andrew threw an arm around her. "It does, but just think of the beautiful pottery you're being made into."

Andrew found Phoebe sitting on the side of the bed, not moving. He looked around. She hadn't packed anything. He sat beside her, finally reaching for her hand.

"Phoebe?"

"I'm not leaving, Andrew. Let's face them here."

"Phoebe? I can understand your reasoning, but we have no idea who's out there or how far they will go."

"I know, Andrew, but I hate this. We already tried running and they still found us. Can you guarantee they won't again?"

Andrew shot a look over his shoulder at Richard who had paused at the door. Richard nodded and moved on.

"None of can do that, Phoebe. It's a calculated risk wherever we go. Richard has a place he can keep us as safe as he can."

Phoebe shook her head. "You have no idea what I lived with those few weeks, Andrew. I can't even really remember them. You also have no idea how restricted my life was before that. I had no freedom. I had no friends. And I know it was Mom who made sure I got a job she could control." She looked up. "I'm finally free of all that. I can have friends, Andrew. Do you know how precious that is? I have your Mom and Dad to love me. And I have you." She stared at him, tears sparkling in her eyes. "I don't want anything to happen to us, but I just can't leave our home."

Andrew wrapped her in a hug and just sat, digesting what she had said. He finally dropped a kiss on her forehead and then rose. "I'll be back."

He went to find Richard, who stood just outside the door.

"I wasn't meaning to eavesdrop, Andrew."

"I know you weren't. But what do we do?"

Richard stared around him, then motioned for Andrew to follow him. "I think we can make this work. You have a good alarm system. If we put in a few more motion sensor lights and outdoor cameras, we should be fine. My team stays with Phoebe. You have a driver back and forth and wherever you go."

Andrew nodded thoughtfully. "That could work. I hear what Phoebe's saying, but it still worries me."

"It would me too, Andrew. Listen, let me talk it over with my team and see what we can come up with. We'd have to have one in the house and one outside at all times."

Andrew nodded once again. "I know, but if it's what we have to do, we have to." He returned to the bedroom, where he found Phoebe folding clothes into one of the dressers. "Richard thinks we can make it work to stay here."

She nodded, her eyes on her work. Andrew hesitated, then moved to stand beside her, his hand going out to sweep her hair back.

"Talk to me, Phoebe. Please don't shut me out."

She looked up, an unreadable look on her face. "What do you want me to say, Andrew? You've made the plans and haven't included me. I feel like this is just a concession, that tomorrow or the next day I'll be swept up and put somewhere under lock and key."

Andrew sighed and then blew out a breath. "You're right, Phoebe. That's what it seems like, but you need to trust that we have your life in our hands. I don't want to lose you. The guys and the ladies on the force? They don't want that either. Work with us."

*Chapter 20*

$\mathcal{A}$ week later, Andrew looked through the paperwork on his desk and sighed. Another late night by the looks of it. He stared at the wall, then down at his desk, before picking up the first file. He read for a moment, then dropped it, rising to go find Bill.

"Bill?" He waited for Bill to turn from his computer. "I've had a thought. Where are we with finding Phoebe's birth parents?"

"We're trying to trace them, but it's like they disappeared into thin air."

"I was afraid of that, Bill. I think they've been gotten out of the way."

Bill sat back, his left hand rubbing the back of his neck. "That's what we're thinking. Lily's heading that way tomorrow to see what she can find out in person. Jason's with her."

Andrew nodded. "What about her sisters' husbands? What do we have on them?"

Bill held up a file. "This is all on them. Thick, isn't it?"

"How close are you to arrest warrants?"

"Almost there. Your parents are still throwing information at us. How do they find this stuff?"

Andrew grinned. "I have no idea. They have contacts all over the place." He sobered. "We need this over, Bill. Who else are we looking at?"

Bill hesitated, his eyes on the folder. "More than who we have been." He looked up at Andrew, his eyes sad. "We've had to start looking at her parents' siblings as well. There are some involved."

"What about the police chief? He's her cousin."

"Now, he's clean. Somehow, he missed out on what's been going on in the family, as did his brothers. There seems to have been some sort of rift between the parents."

"That's good, I guess. Phoebe hasn't talked much about her aunts, uncles or cousins."

"No, I don't expect she would have. By the sounds of it, she didn't have much contact with them. From what we're hearing from old staff at her parents', she was kept pretty much isolated from everyone. It's a wonder she's turned out as well as she has."

"I know. She's got some issues we're working through. Trust is one. She also has a very low self-esteem." Andrew sat back, his face thoughtful. "Bill, do we need to set up a sting or anything like that?"

"I don't think we will. With the evidence the team's finding we should be able to get arrest warrants without any difficulty, I'm thinking by the end of the week at the latest. I've talked to Judge Lane and he's ready to authorize them when they're ready." He paused, not quite sure how to continue. "The thing of it is, who don't we arrest?"

Andrew stared at him, then gave a bark of laughter. "It's that bad?" At Bill's nod, he shook his head. "I didn't realize it was that bad. I've stayed away as much as I can from the investigation, so as not to taint it."

"I know you have. The prosecuting attorney and the judges know that as well." Bill stood and paced. "We need to keep

Phoebe out of sight for the next week. Can Richard do that?”

“I’m sure he can. She’s starting to get cabin fever, but Silver on Richard’s team has some ideas on what to do. One of them is redecorating the kitchen.”

“Are you serious?” When Andrew just looked at him, he laughed. “I hope you have some say in it.”

Andrew shook his head, a smile on his face. “Phoebe has great colour sense. I trust her. You haven’t seen what she did to my office?” Andrew pulled out his phone and brought up a picture.

“That’s your office now? Wow! We need her in here.”

Andrew laughed as he stood. “Keep me updated as you can, without compromising what you’re doing. I’m cutting out soon. I have a meeting with the mayor at 4 and then I’m off home. Do you need anything?”

Bill shook his head. “No. We’re good. Your aunt’s been providing meals for us, so that has been a blessing.”

“Auntie Ev? I didn’t know that.”

✳ ✳ ✳ ✳ ✳

Silver, one of Richard's female team members, stopped at the kitchen door, a smile on her face. Stephen, one of her coworkers, sat at the kitchen table, a look on his face that said he was up to no good. Phoebe was laughing at something he said. Silver walked by, ruffling his hair.

"Hey! Don't mess with the coif!" Stephen tried to straighten out his unruly curls with no success.

"Coif?" Silver started to laugh. "Where did you come up with that word?"

"My grandmother. It was one of her favourite words." Stephen looked between the two women. "Something tells me you two are up to something."

"Really, Stephen? You have to repeat yourself?" Silver's eyes sparkled as she shared a look with Phoebe.

"I didn't repeat myself." Stephen stopped, remembering what he said, and groaned. "I did, didn't I? Now do you ladies need anything lifted or moved? If not, I'm heading out."

"We're good, I think, Stephen. Thanks for asking," Phoebe stood and moved towards the counter. "Silver, if we tape garbage bags over the window glass, will that suffice while we paint the trim?"

"It should." Silver stared around. "You would think we'd be making a real mess, painting the walls and the cupboards, but you have it down to a science of unmessinesss. How do you do that?"

Phoebe shrugged. "Just organized, I guess. I had lots of time to daydream as a kid, with nothing else I was allowed to do."

Silver spun to stare at her, not realizing what kind of an upbringing she had had. "Well, let's get messy then. I hear tell your husband won't be home until after 6. He has a meeting with the mayor."

Phoebe sighed. "He does. I wish this was over, Silver. I'm tired of living like this. It's been my whole life. I had a taste of freedom, you know, and liked it."

Silver nodded. "Well, Bill and his team are working hard on that. Trust me. You'll be free soon enough."

＊ ＊ ＊ ＊ ＊

Hanging up his phone, Bill stared at it and then at the door. He sighed and rose. He needed to let Andrew know what Lily and Jason had dug up. It wasn't good news.

"Andrew? Got a moment?" Bill had tracked him down at the front desk.

Andrew shot him a look, then pointed towards his office. "Go on in. I'll be right there." Andrew turned back to finish going over the paperwork with the officer at the desk, then turned. His heart was heavy. He could read Bill well after working with him for years, and he knew Bill did not have good news for him.

He shut the door before sinking into his chair. He felt old today, old and weary.

"What do you have for me, Bill?"

Bill shook his head. "I just got off the phone with Lily. She and Jason are still digging, but Phoebe's biological mom is dead and her father is missing. She has a sister, a couple of years younger Lily said."

"This isn't good." Andrew buried his head in his hands. "How do I tell her this after she has gotten her hopes up?"

"That's not the worst of it. We think her mom was murdered and her dad was as well."

Andrew's head shot up. "Her biological parents?" At Bill's nod, he shook his head. "This just gets worse and worse, doesn't it? I guessing this was done to hide the fact Phoebe was stolen?"

"We're tracking that down. Lily's talked to your Mom."

"Good. Listen, when you have all the facts, I'm going to have to talk to Phoebe."

"No, Andrew. Let me. It's better if it comes from someone other than you."

Andrew stared at his friend, then slowly nodded. "I guess." He shot a look at the clock and then his desk. "Listen, I think I'm going to head home. I need to spend some time with Phoebe."

"I'll get your driver. Andrew?" When Andrew looked up, Bill was staring at him. "Lily did mention the possibility that her mom's death and her dad's disappearance was faked. The sister isn't saying much. Lily's made arrangements for her to disappear as well."

"Good. Thank you. Pass my thanks to Lily as well."

*  *  *  *  *

Phoebe turned as she heard footsteps heading her way. Andrew stood in the door way, eyeing the kitchen. Richard had warned him as he came in that the ladies had been at work.

"Andrew?" Phoebe's voice was hesitant.

"Phoebe? Leave you for a day and this is the result?" Andrew raised an eyebrow, then smiled. "I like it."

"You do?" She stood before him, still not sure.

"I really do, love. It's great. It's so you." Andrew reached for her hand. "I need to talk to you, Phoebe. Come with me for a moment."

He seated her on the side of the bed and then sat beside her, a troubled look on his face.

"Andrew?"

"Phoebe, Lily has been to interview the people you tracked down. She talked to the daughter and then had her put into protective custody. She can't find the parents."

"What? Can't find them?"

Andrew shook his head, then pulled out his phone. "She sent me pictures. I shouldn't be showing them to you, but I will. You need to trust us on this, though."

She nodded, watching as he handed her his phone. She stared at it in a puzzled manner. "Are you sure these are the right people?"

"Why?"

"I look nothing like them. Eye colour. Hair colour. Skin tone. Nothing matches."

Andrew sighed. "That's what I thought. Lily's still there, digging deeper into the family."

"Andrew, when does it stop and we can go on with life?"

"Soon, I pray, Phoebe."

She stood and paced, arms crossed across her body. "You keep telling me that, Andrew, but it just keeps going on. How soon?"

Andrew watched her, a shadow on his. face. He knew how long some of these investigations took. "I don't know, Phoebe. That's the thing with investigations. Sometimes they go cold and we never solve them. We're working really hard to solve this. We're close to making arrests and serving warrants, but we need some key pieces of information yet."

Sitting back down beside Andrew, Phoebe eyed the pictures again, lost in thought. "Andrew, when was that put up on the adoptions website?"

Andrew stared at her. "What are you thinking, Phoebe?"

"I'm thinking someone did this to try and find me. That is was a bogus listing."

Andrew nodded. "I think I see where you're going with this. Let me talk to Bill in the morning. First though, I hear Richard ordered pizza since the kitchen was torn up earlier."

Phoebe signed and leaned against Andrew's shoulder. "He did, did he? I'm really not hungry tonight, Andrew. All this has sort of taken away my appetite."

"One piece, Phoebe. That's all I ask is that you eat one piece."

# Chapter 21

_Lily was on a mission. She needed to find Bill and couldn't. She stopped, her eyes going towards Andrew's door, then back towards Bill's. She turned, finding him standing right behind her.

"Lily? I didn't expect you back yet." Cup of coffee in hand, he pointed to his office.

"I didn't expect to be. I needed to talk with you about what I found."

Bill searched her face. "This doesn't sound good."

Lily shook her head. "It's not. The listing on the website was a dummied up one. It's been pulled. I have our computer tech searching for where is originated." She paused, not quite sure how to proceed.

"They're not Phoebe's family."

She shook her head. "You were right. They're not. We have found the older couple and the younger woman and arrested them. Whoever hired them, and they're not talking, was trying to flush out Phoebe."

Bill sat back, eyes on Lily. "Then, how did they know she was searching websites like that?"

"Our tech thinks they've buried a program on her computer."

Bill nodded, his eyes shifting to the doorway where he could see activity going on. "Lily, head for the board room. Put up what you have on the whiteboards and then we'll work it through. We're getting close and they're getting desperate."

"I know they are. Andrew talked to Phoebe last night."

"About?"

"The adoption and lost children websites. She's agreed to stay away from them for now, until we get this all sorted out."

Bill nodded. "I figured he would. Did he show her pictures as well?"

Lily shrugged. "I suspect he has. He asked for copies so he could show Richard and his team, just in case they showed up at the house."

* * * * *

Phoebe sat, her eyes on the closed drapes in the living room, thoughts miles from where she was. Lord, I have no idea what's going on, but You do. Lead Bill and his team to the answers soon, please? I need my freedom. I know You are making me into a new person, but does it have to be like this?

Richard watched, eyes compassionate as he studied her face. He sighed heavily before coming and sitting facing her.

"Phoebe?" He waited until she looked at him. "What can we do to make it easier for you?"

She shrugged. "I really don't know, Richard. This is what I have lived with all my life. No freedom. No choice. Alone. No friends. Family that avoided me unless absolutely necessary."

Richard winced. "You don't pull your punches any more, do you?" She stared at him. "Look, Phoebe. None of us like this any more than you do, but we need to keep you safe. Andrew has asked if we can make arrangements for him to take you out to dinner tonight. We're working on it. It will have to be somewhere small."

"Like his Auntie Ev's diner?"

Richard nodded. "Like that. His cousin is there today, so that will help."

She sighed. "I hate doing this to you, putting you and your team at risk."

Richard gave a small laugh as he shrugged. "It's what we do, Phoebe. It's our job. Now, what can we do today to make it easier for you? Any painting projects?"

She shook her head. "No. What I would really like to do is research the college here in town. Is that too much to ask?"

Richard shook his head. "No. I can get Silver to bring in a laptop and you two can work away at it. Anything in particular you're looking at?"

She shook her head. "Not really. I wasn't allowed to go to college. I was put into that job as soon as I finished high school and hated every moment of it. I just want to see what options I have out there."

"Do you draw?"

She shook her head. "Not talented that way. Maybe I should just write my life story as a novel. No one would ever believe it though."

Richard started laughing. "It would make a good suspense book, wouldn't it?"

"That's what I feel like I'm living right now. I want to read that final chapter and know it's over."

* * * * *

Bill hung up his phone and then reaching for his jacket, hit the door on the run, searching for his team. Andrew stood watching.

"Bill?"

"We just got word that your house has been compromised, Andrew. Let's move."

Andrew stared at him, then hit the outside door on a run.

"Have you called Richard?"

"Lily did. She was heading that way already." Bill hit the lights and sirens as he left the parking lot. "How did they do that, Andrew?"

"I have no idea. Richard and his team are too good. It was likely they've been watching the house, waiting for a chance to get to her." Andrew prayed like he had never prayed before, his heart quaking at the thought of something happening to his Phoebe.

Bill slowed to a halt as he saw the street blocked off. Andrew searched for Richard's vehicles and couldn't see them.

"Where are they, Bill?" Andrew stood at the barricade, his head swivelling as he searched the area.

Bill turned in a circle. "They're not here, Andrew." He reached for his phone. "Richard? You're safe? I'll let him know. He's with me."

Andrew had turned as Bill talked. "They're safe?"

Bill nodded. "Just let me check into something, Andrew. Then we'll go. I know as police chief you need to know what's going on, but you're also involved as a victim here too. How do we investigate and keep you out of it?"

Andrew blew out a breath. "That's a good question, Bill. I don't have an answer for that."

"I don't either. Thank goodness the prosecutor is aware of what's going on."

Andrew nodded, then turning back to his house, spoke. "Where are they, Bill?"

"Richard didn't say. Just asked we meet you at your aunt's diner."

Andrew shot him a look, then nodded. "That means he's gotten Avery involved, then."

Bill stopped, starting at Andrew. "Avery? Why?"

"Federal crimes are involved, so I would gather he wants federal protection." Andrew dug his hands into his pockets, lost in thought. "I'm not ready for that, Bill. Nor will Phoebe be. I can't pull her from here, where she's had some sense of normalcy and stick her away in a safe house somewhere."

"And if you don't, you might not survive. A dilemma there, my friend." Bill walked away. In short order he was back, pointing to his vehicle. "Do you need to go back to the department?"

"I should. I need paperwork from there to work on, if I'm not going to be going there tomorrow."

Bill nodded. "Let's get your paperwork, then, and get you to your lady."

Andrew watched his town pass by as Bill drove him towards his aunt's diner. Where did I go wrong, Lord, that I placed Phoebe in danger? Or is the other way? I don't want to lose her, Lord, and I certainly don't want to walk away from my calling. You've placed me where You want me. Give me peace this day, please, dear Lord.

Phoebe turned as she heard the diner door open. Stephen kept his hand on her arm to keep her from rushing across the room to Andrew.

"Let him come to you, Phoebe. We have you where we can keep you safe right now." Stephen's voice was quiet enough that only Phoebe heard him.

She nodded. "I hate this, Stephen. When do I get freedom again?"

"I understand it's almost wrapped up, Phoebe, but this is the dangerous point of any investigation or protection detail." Richard sat on her other side. He rose as Andrew approached.

Andrew stopped before he reached her, an inscrutable look on his face, before he turned to Bill. In a quiet voice, he spoke. "Bill, I need you to investigate someone, by yourself, without involving anyone else."

Bill was puzzled but agreed. "Who?"

"Dad's secretary, Mary." At Bill's shocked look, Andrew spoke quickly. "It's all too coincidental, Bill. How do they know where we are? Why me? Why not someone else?"

"I get where you're coming from. I'll look into it as soon as we're done."

Andrew thanked him. "And keep it between us two, please."

"That I will." Bill nodded towards Phoebe. "Now, go find your wife. I think I need to run over some plans with Richard."

"Just keep me in the loop, Bill. I'm not sitting back any more." Andrew walked towards Phoebe, leaving Bill staring after him.

Richard stood beside Bill, watching the table where his team sat.

"Now what, Bill?"

Bill shrugged. "I have a feeling Andrew's ready to go on the offensive. He's not willing to hide anymore. And somehow I don't think Phoebe is either."

"No, neither of them are. So, where do we put them? I can't take them back to Andrew's."

Bill shook his head. "What kind of place are you looking for, Richard?"

"Somewhere it would be difficult to track them, but keep them close to town. And don't say the cabin. I've checked it out. Not a place to keep very safe."

"No, it's not. Let me think for a moment." Bill turned and paced out of the diner, spinning when he heard steps approaching him.

"Bill?  I'm Avery, Andrew's cousin. How can I help?"

"Your cousin is ready to fight and we can't have that."

Avery broke into laughter.  "You have no idea how ready he is to fight.  I've never seen him like this before, and I've seen him angry in the past.  I don't think you have, even though you've been friends for years."

"No, I haven't.  He's usually the voice of reason."

Avery laughed again.  "That's a good way to describe him.  Listen, I know of a place."  He held up his hands.  "Not a safe house, but it could very easily be.  Jonah's."

"Jonah's?"  Bill shook his head.  "He has a farm.  How safe is that?"

It was Avery's turn to shake his head. "Not the farm.  Not many people know he has a house down the road from there.  It's not in his name, so we could get away with it.  I'm sure they've done all this research on his friends and found every house or apartment any of us have lived in."

Bill nodded.  "Do you break it to him or not?"

"Let me talk to Richard first.  And here he is."

The three men stood, deep in discussion, eyes watching Andrew and Phoebe. They finally walked towards the diner door, a plan in place.

Andrew stood as they approached him, eyes narrowed as he searched their faces. He sighed. He knew he wasn't going to like what they had to say, and he doubted Phoebe would either.

"Well, where are we heading now?" Andrew's question stopped them in their tracks.

"We have a house we can use."

Phoebe stood, hands on her hips, and shook her head. "No. The only place I'm heading is home." She brushed by them and was out of the diner before they could stop her, Stephen at her heels.

Andrew shook his head, a smile on his face. "And did you three really think you would get her away from there?" He walked rapidly after her.

The three stood, staring after them, then at each other.

"What just happened?" Bill asked.

Avery started to laugh. "That's Andrew, Bill. If you didn't know before, you know now. He has never ever backed down from a fight, particularly if it involves someone he cares about." He pointed at Phoebe. "And that woman there has his heart. He'll do everything in his power to protect her."

Richard sighed, knowing they had to approach them once more. "They do make it difficult for us, don't they?" He eyed the other two men. "Which one of you wants to talk to them?"

Avery held up his hands, as he watched Andrew turn to face the diner. "Not me. I know Andrew too well. Unless Phoebe agrees to go to a safe house, they're not going."

They once more approached Andrew and Phoebe. Phoebe stood in the circle of Andrew's arm, her face unreadable, but her hands were tight on Andrew's arm. Andrew just watched silently, his mind racing as to where they would be safe. He knew of a place they could go do, but somehow he didn't think Richard would want to.

"So, where are you putting us?" Phoebe's voice broke the silence, resignation evident in hit.

"We have a house just outside town, Phoebe. It's in the country, lots of good visibility around it."

Andrew shook his head.  "If it's connected to someone I know, I can guarantee you they'll know about it.  Doesn't matter if it is in that person's name or not."

Avery studied his cousin's face. "You're right, Andrew.  But where?"

Andrew shared a look with Avery, who then nodded.  "I know where you're thinking, Andrew.  Why didn't I think of that?"

Andrew laughed.  "You think too much of safe houses and that kind of stuff, cuz. You've forgotten to think like I do."

Avery laughed as well.  "That's so true. Bill.  Richard.  Trust him on this one.  They'll be tucked away in plain sight."

$\mathscr{B}$ill and Richard stared around the campground Andrew had directed them to. He had made them exchange the newer vehicles for older models, and Stephen wasn't happy about that.

"Really, Andrew?  A campground?" Richard turned in a circle, eyeing the area around him.

"Would you think to look here?" Andrew stood, eyes watchful.

"I won't, that's for sure."  Richard nodded. "This has possibilities.  A number of ways in and out.  Hard to cover them all, but if we stay tight to the cabins, we should be okay."  He turned as Silver approached.

"We're set, Richard.  Thank goodness the campground was empty."

Andrew laughed at the expression of Silver's face. "Not a camper, Silver?  You'll find the cabins quite comfortable.  And Bill has promised it's only for a day or two. Now, if you'll excuse me, I need to go find my wife."

They watched Andrew walk away, then turned to one another.

"Are you okay with this, Richard? I can pull rank or something." Bill spoke quietly.

"I am for now, but we need to be ready to move quickly. Silver, make sure the vehicles are positioned in that way. Stephen and Timothy are walking the perimeter right now, determining the second and third routes of escape."

Naomi walked from the cabin Andrew and Phoebe would be using and headed towards Richard.

"Which cabin do you want to set up as the dining cabin?"

"Try the one beside Andrew's. We'll use it for you two ladies. Timothy and Stephen will take the one on the other side."

"And which one will you take?"

Richard pointed. "I'll take the one right across from them. We can set up our surveillance in there."

Andrew approached them as they stood talking and waited for Richard to speak.

“Andrew?”

“Yeah, Richard. What are your plans? I know you have some. I need to do some work and that I have to take into town tomorrow.”

Richard ran his hands down his face. “We can’t keep going back and forth, Andrew. They’ll spot us.”

“I have no choice about this, Richard. I am the police chief and as such has duties I have to take care of. Bill can act in my spot in an emergency but he’s deep into multiple investigations, not just this one.”

Richard stared at him for a moment. “I get that, Andrew, and we’ll get you back and forth as safely as we can. We just need to keep it to a minimum.”

“I get that too, Richard. Don’t interfere with my position, that’s all I’m saying.” Andrew turned and stood away.

“Well, I guess you got told.” Silver’s voice held a tone of amusement.

“Not funny, Silver.” Richard’s voice was resigned.

“I know it’s not, but I can see it from his point of view, can’t you?”

Richard nodded, then turned to Bill. “You staying the night or heading back in?”

"I'm heading back in. Andrew's asked me to investigate something for him."

✳ ✳ ✳ ✳ ✳

Phoebe watched as Andrew paced the small living area in the cabin. The curtains were drawn tight, and he had turned on the heat just enough to take off the dampness and the chill. She rested her chin on her drawn-up knees, arms wrapped around her legs, and then finally spoke.

"Andrew?"

He turned, a smile crossing his face, before he came and sat, his arm drawing her close. "Phoebe? Are you okay out here?"

"We have to be somewhere. I'd rather be at home."

"It's home now, is it?"

She poked him, then nodded. "It is, Andrew. I've never really had a home before, not like you have." She studied his face. "Where does the investigation stand?"

"About where it was last night. I've asked Bill to run one more name for me."

"I'm not even going to ask." Her head went down on his shoulder. "Any idea how long we'll be in the boonies?"

"The boonies, is it?" He started to laugh at the expression on her face. "I have no idea, love. Bill's working the investigation, and he hasn't told me."

"I want it over with, Drew. They've taken enough of my life."

Andrew's eyes studied her face. He noticed she was calling him Drew more and more. He liked that. Then he sighed. They couldn't have a normal life until this was over. Please, Lord, let it be soon.

Phoebe's breath softened and her body relaxed as she drifted off to sleep. Andrew reached for a blanket he had left on the couch and used it to cover her. His own head went back, and he too slept. He didn't hear the soft ticking and clicking coming from his briefcase. Neither of them did.

The man watching from the forest nodded, then turned and walked away, heading for his vehicle. The security men hadn't seen him, he knew. He had kept too well hidden. Soon, he thought. Soon, he would have those two in his control. If not in his control, then dead. And if dead, then the investigations would stop, right? That's what he had promised.

✳ ✳ ✳ ✳ ✳

Andrew stretched the next morning, working out the kinks in his neck. He had carried Phoebe to their bed in the middle of the night and then returned to the couch, watchful for the rest of the night. He paused as he reached for his briefcase. Something stopped him. Then he opened it, his hands running through it. He stopped, eyes sliding closed. How had they managed that? He turned at the tap at the door, reaching to open in and usher in Richard.

"This is how, Richard. I've been carrying a tracker with me."

Richard's face whitened. "Then they know where we are. How did that get in there?"

"I have no idea. I lock it at work and at home when I close it. Someone has had to pick it."

Richard nodded, then sighed. "That's means this is not a good hiding place either. Now where?"

Andrew shrugged. "I have no idea, Richard. I would say we stay here and defend ourselves. Phoebe won't move to another house."

"I know she won't and she has to."

"I have to what?" Phoebe stood, eyes steady on the two men. "Did I understand you to say that we've been found again?"

"Not yet, not that we know of. But we could have been."

"I'm not moving again, Richard. This is it. Either that or you take us home." She spun, Andrew catching a look of tears in her eyes.

Richard drew a deep breath. "How far along is the investigation again?"

"Almost complete, I think, Richard. Bill said two days ago it would only be a couple of days."

Richard nodded. "Then we hunker down here. If needed, Don Adams said he would help, but I'd rather not bring in someone new to add to the mix."

"Do what you think is best. I need to go into town, but I don't want to any more." Andrew walked away to find his wife.

Richard nodded, then turned to find his team. They needed to do more planning.

✳ ✳ ✳ ✳ ✳

Bill turned as he heard his voice call. Amos was there. Just the person he didn't want to see.

"Amos?  What brings you here?"

"Andrew.  Have you seen him in the last couple of days?"

"Why?"

"I'm getting worried.  He's not answering his voice mail messages." Amos' eyes were narrowed as he watched Bill's reaction.

"He's been busy, Amos. He's got a lot of paperwork and budget stuff he's having to take care off."

Amos snorted.  "There's more to it than that, isn't there?'

Bill finally nodded and then spoke. "Why, Amos?"

"Why what?"

"Why'd you betray Andrew like that? You have no wife, no kids.  You've never let him visit you in all these years, feeding him lies about your family."

"What are you talking about?"

Bill held up a folder.  "This, Amos. I've been investigating you, at Andrew's request.  I am placing you under arrest for attempted murder, conspiracy to commit murder, fraud.  That's just for starters."

Amos stared at him and then sneered. "Think you have it all figured out? You don't. Not by a long shot."

Bill nodded to the officer standing behind Amos. "Take him away. And just for the record, Amos, we know a lot more than you would expect us to find out. I know about your parents and their little games. I know about how you ingratiated yourself with the Knights. The police chief in your town was very helpful. He's been watching you for a while now, waiting until he had enough to arrest you. He'll be bringing officers to take you back to your town. It's won't go well with you, I can guarantee you that. Your so-called friends will turn on you in an instant." Bill walked away, knowing he had to call Andrew and let him know the outcome of the investigation.

∗ ∗ ∗ ∗ ∗

Andrew turned as he heard Richard approaching, pocketing his phone. He had just spoken with Bill and he needed to vent.

"Andrew?"

"Yeah, Richard?"

"Are you okay?" Richard's eyes held concern.

"No, I'm not, actually. Just found out a friend was selling us out. The one who asked me to go in and bring Phoebe out. Bill completed an investigation on him and then arrested him this morning."

"That sucks. Now what?"

Andrew shook his head. "I have no idea what's happening now. Bill said he'd be in touch." Andrew looked around the campground. "How safe are we really, Richard?"

Richard shrugged. "I have no idea, Andrew. There's someone out there. The guys have found evidence of that."

"So, we're being watched."

"It would appear so. Are you still heading into town?"

Andrew nodded. "I need to. There's things I can't leave to anyone else."

"Then I suggest we all head in there. Is there a room we can tuck away in at the department?"

Andrew nodded. "We have a small boardroom that would work. We're using the conference room right now for a couple of investigations. Let's move. I'd like to be out of here sooner than later."

* * * * *

Phoebe paced the small room, feeling claustrophobic. She knew Silver and Stephen had to stay with her, but she wanted Andrew there as well. She knew he couldn't be though. She turned as the door opened and Richard entered, bags of takeout food in his hands.

"Evie sent food for us, guys. Let's eat. Andrew will be here shortly. I understand he's about done for the day, so we'll be heading out shortly."

"Where to now, Richard? It seems everywhere we go they find us."

"I know they do. Andrew has come up with a plan. I'm not keen on it, but he and Bill think it will work. And no, we're not about to tell you what it is." Richard grinned at the disgruntled look on Phoebe's face. "We'll tell you as we need to."

Andrew stood in the doorway and watched as Phoebe pushed her food around on the plate. He was worried. She wasn't eating and he knew he needed, somehow, to get her to eat. Lord, how do I do it? How do I take care of her?

He turned away for a moment, not quite sure how to proceed. Then, turning back, he saw Phoebe watching him, a look on her face that said she trusted him totally. How did she read him like that already? He nodded, then entered to room to sit beside her, pushing her plate back towards her.

"Eat, love. I don't know when we'll eat again."

She searched his face and then nodded. "I will if you will."

He reached for the plate Silver handed him. "Eat. Then we talk and make plans."

Andrew finally sat back, wiping his mouth and hands with a paper napkin. He searched the faces of Richard's team and then sought Phoebe's face. Her eyes were focused on the plate of food she had barely touched. Bill, he knew, stood in the doorway, an unhappy look on his face.

Andrew cleared his throat, and all eyes were on him in a flash. "Listen, people. We've been through some rough parts but this is where the rubber meets the road. This is where it gets interesting. I have a plan and we'll see if it flushes out our opponents."

Richard shook his head when he heard the plan once more. "It won't work, Andrew. There is no way it will work."

Andrew stared at him, then grinned. "You come up with a plan, then, and we'll see which one does work."

"A dare, is it now? Do I get to work with my team?"

Andrew shook his head. "Nope. I didn't, so you don't."

Richard glared at him, then looked down, lost in thought. He finally shook his head, conceding that Andrew just may have come up with the right plan.

"So, I guess it's your plan, Andrew. When do we move out?"

"Shortly. Bill's is just finalized off some details." He looked around the room. "I understand if you want to pull your team, Richard."

The five team members stared at him and then at each other, all shaking their heads.

"Not happening, Andrew. We're in to the finish," Richard stood and began gathering up the remnants of their meal.

* * * * *

Richard headed towards the house the team had stopped in front of, a bungalow with a detached garage. He didn't like this. Where had Andrew come up with this house?

219

He nodded to Timothy and Naomi as they spread out to search and then secure the area. What he did like was that the house sat in the middle of a lot, no trees or shrubs or outbuildings close to the house.

He finally returned to the van, opening the door and staring at Andrew.

"Well?" Andrew waited for Richard to speak.

Richard shook his head. "Where did you come up with this, Andrew?"

"It belongs to the grandparents of a friend from elementary school. They moved here years ago and there should be no connection between us and them. Using this type of van makes it look as if the family are here. It's similar enough the neighbours won't say anything."

"And you think we'll be safe here for a few days?" Richard watched the conflicting emotions crossing Phoebe's face.

"Bill says he'll be making the final arrests within twenty-four hours. That's all the time we need. And who would look for us here in Phoebe's hometown?"

Phoebe's eyes shot to Andrew's as he turned to her. "Why, Andrew? Why come back here?"

"Because we need to, love. We need to finish it off where it started, right here."

"No, it didn't start in this town. It started somewhere else."

"No, it's here we make our stand, love."

# Chapter 23

*B*ill pocketed his phone, a thoughtful look on his face. He headed to find his team, ready to send them out with the warrants. He stood for a moment, watching the last-minute activity in the boardroom, before searching out Lily.

"Do you have enough detectives here to head out?"

Lily turned, nodding. "We actually have more than we need. I spoke with the chief in Phoebe's town. They're ready to move at the same time we are."

"Good. Listen. I need you and Jason to come with me. I'm heading towards Andrew. Something tells me we're going to be needed there."

Lily searched the room and waved Jason over. "Okay, then, we're ready to move."

Jason headed a stack of folders to Bill. "I'll drive. You read."

"What is this?"

"The tail-end of the investigation. This brings it all together. Phoebe had good instincts about her family." Jason pointed to the folder. "It's all in there, Bill. I don't think we realized how big a deal it was."

* * * * *

Andrew sat, watching Stephen as he worked away on a laptop. He finally stood and paced, finding himself in the kitchen. Silver stood at the sink, veggies surrounding it, as she worked to prepare a meal.

"You don't have to cook for us, Silver. There's plenty of canned goods."

She turned, a smile on her face. "It's what I do to unwind, Andrew. Cook. My friends are always glad to be recipients of what I prepare."

"It smells delicious, whatever you have on the stove there."

She grinned at him. "Not telling you yet, Andrew. It's a surprise for supper."

He nodded, a smile creasing through the grim lines on his face. "I guess I'll have to wait just like everyone else. Have you seen Phoebe?"

"I think Naomi had her downstairs in the exercise room. Who would have thought a house like this would have all the modern conveniences?"

Andrew laughed as he turned for the basement stairs. "It's just who these people are. They're into healthy living, including exercise, and provided that gym downstairs for their kids and grandkids and their friends. It's what they've always done."

Andrew approached Phoebe, resting a hand on her shoulder. "Had enough, love?"

She looked up at him, a frown in place. "Enough what?"

Andrew grinned. "Enough of everything." He pulls out his phone as it chimed, walking away to take the call in private. His eyes lit on Phoebe, before he turned, taking the stairs two at a time and searching for Richard.

"Richard?"

Stephen looked up. "He's outside, Andrew. Do you need him?"

"I do."

"Stay put. I'll be right back."

Richard turned as Stephen walked towards him, his eyes still searching the area. Something was off, he thought, but what?

"Andrew's looking for you, Richard. I'll stay here. You go talk to him."

Richard nodded. "I feel something, Stephen, and I have no idea what."

Stephen agreed. "I have since we got here. I know there are plain clothes officers stationed around, but I think we're not done yet."

"I don't either. Be back shortly."

Andrew turned as Richard approached. "Richard? I just got word from Bill. They've served all the warrants and made their arrests."

Richard drew a sigh of relief. "Did they get everyone?"

"He said to give them another twenty-four to forty-eight hours. I'm pushing for the twenty-four."

Richard turned to search his face. "I'm thinking it will be a bit longer. Did they get the head one?"

"That we don't know yet. Somehow, I'm not sure that we have. Let's make some plans, Richard. I know you're in charge, but I want to be part of the planning."

"As would I, if the roles were reversed."

* * * * *

Early the next morning, Bill walked into the house, interrupting their breakfast. Phoebe stared at him, a forkful of pancakes halfway to her mouth. Andrew's arm came around her as he waited for Bill to speak.

"I think it's safe enough for you to go back to your home, Andrew, Phoebe. Richard's going to stay for a couple of days, just until we ensure we have everyone."

"Can you tell us about it, please, Bill?" Phoebe's voice was low and uncertain.

Bill accepted the mug of coffee and the plate of food he was handed and stood by the counter, eyes down for a moment. He finally looked up, meeting Andrew's eyes. Andrew nodded, knowing that what was coming would be hard on Phoebe.

"Phoebe, this is not easy, you know? We've arrested your parents, your sisters, their husbands. Your nieces and nephew are now with their paternal grandparents. Your father was a leader in money laundering for a large group of business owners. He used the factory where you worked, which he owned by the way, to send packages of money and drugs overseas. We found the overseas accounts they set up. Did you know there was a whole building set up to manufacture drugs?"   When she shook her head, he continued, "I didn't think you did. Everyone said you never went out to on the floor, that you stayed in your office area all the time. Can you tell me why?"

She shrugged. "I had no need to go out there. Besides, you needed a pass card to get out there and I was never given one. Mother made sure of that."

Bill nodded. "That's what she said. The thing of it is, none of them are sorry. None of them want to see you. I'm sorry, Phoebe, that it turned out this way."

She just shook her head. "It's the way it's always been, Bill. I've never been a true part of the family, always an outsider." She stopped, her eyes searching Andrew's. "Did you ever get to the bottom of the missing children website?"

Andrew spoke. "We did. Stephen here did the research on it. The listing for a child matching your description was bogus on that one."

She frowned. "On that one? What do you mean?"

"What it means, Phoebe, is that you really are a missing child. That you never belonged to that family. We're still working through the hows and whys."   Stephen watched with compassion as her hand flew to her mouth. "What we have determined is that you were stolen from your family as a two-year-old. We gather that your father had seen something he shouldn't have and you were taken in retaliation. Lily has made first contact with your family. Your parents, your sister, your two brothers. She's got the information you need. All they've been told for now is that you are still alive but have been put into protective custody because of an investigation. Your hometown is Grenville."

"So close." Phoebe's eyes filled with tears before she burrowed her head into Andrew's chest, his arms cradling her close.

"So close, love. We'll reach out to them once we know we're safe." He looked up at Bill, then Stephen. "Thank you both for what you have done for Phoebe."

There was silence in the room for a while. Then, Richard stood. "I guess we can head back to your place now, Andrew. Let's get this show on the road."

Andrew stood talking with Richard, watching Phoebe as she and Stephen walked towards one of the vans. He turned to a circle, feeling uncomfortable.

"Something wrong, Andrew?" Richard watched his friend.

"There is, Richard. Someone's here. Who did we not arrest?"

Andrew spun and hit the ground, a searing pain in his thigh. Richard landed next to him, weapon out and raised, searching the area, before turning to Andrew.

"Andrew, stay with me, buddy. You've been shot."

Andrew's head raised briefly. "I know. Phoebe."

Richard turned slightly, then ducked as the bullets found the vehicle doors just above them. "Stephen's with her. I think Silver was too. Just lie still."

Andrew groaned as he reached for his thigh. "Is she okay, Richard?"

"She's on the ground, Andrew. I can't tell from here. And I'm not moving until I know it's safe to do so."

Andrew's head went back and his vision darkened. He could faintly hear Richard's voice and the noise and confusion around him before the waves of darkness overtook him totally.

Richard bit back words. How did they find us? The sirens approaching were a welcome sound, but could they catch the shooters?  And there was more than one, he knew.

Bill ran towards Richard in a crouch, his eyes searching the area.  "The officers have the shooters.  How's Andrew?"

"He's down.  The bullet got him in the thigh.  He faded out on me a few minutes okay."  He spun to stare in the direction he knew Phoebe was.  "How's Phoebe?"

Bill shook his head.  "She's been shot at least twice from what Silver said. Stephen's down too."

Richard shared a look with Bill.  "How did they find us?"

Richard watched as the paramedics worked on Andrew before he turned and walked to where Stephen lay.

"How is he?"

The paramedic looked up.  "It grazed his temple, knocked him out.  We'll be moving him soon."  The man shot a look at the paramedics working over Phoebe.

Richard moved closer, watching as the paramedic spun on his knee to rifle through one of his kits and then turn back.  His eyes drawn to Phoebe's face, he winced.  She was pale, almost gray, and he could see her lips turning blue.  Lord, we can't lose her.  We were so close.

"What can we do?"

The other paramedic looked up from where she had been placing an IV and shook her head.  "It's not looking good.  We need an air ambulance."

"They're just about here.  I want one of my guys to ride with you."

They stopped and stared at him before going back to trying to stabilize Phoebe. Silver stood beside Richard and then moved towards the air ambulance, fear briefly crossing her face.  She had come to count on Phoebe as a friend.  Please, Lord, don't let us lose these three.

Richard turned as he heard Bill approaching.

"How's Phoebe?"  Bill's eyes follow the path of the ambulance as it rose into the sky.

"Not looking good, Bill.  I can tell they don't expect her to make it to the hospital."

Bill bit his lip.  "How did they know where you were?"

"Did you find Mary, the secretary?"

Bill stopped. "You know what, we never did. I have officers actively searching for her."

"Find her and I think you'll solve the problem. Somehow, it has to have been someone in law enforcement that sold us out all the time."

Bill nodded. "I agree. Your team's okayed to leave. I'll catch up with you at the hospital."

Richard nodded, his eyes searching for Timothy and Naomi. A sadness rose within him. They had never had this happen before on a security detail. Why this time?

* * * * *

Emily and Simon almost ran through the Emergency Room doors, heading for the clerk. Bill intercepted them.

"Emily. Simon. The doctors are with Andrew right now. They said they'd be out in about 15 minutes."

"How bad, Bill?" Simon ushered his wife to a chair and then sat beside her, her hand tight in his.

"He was shot in the leg and passed out. From what I understand, he's been in and out."

"Phoebe?" Emily's voice held her fear.

Bill shook his head, and her heart fell. "I haven't heard, but Richard said she was hurt pretty bad. I haven't had a chance to talk to anyone about her yet."

"What happened, Bill? I thought they were safe." Simon was trying to understand what had happened and couldn't.

"They should have been. We made all the arrests and then this happened. Someone we didn't know about must have done this. We think it was Mary."

"Mary? Oh no. Why?" Emily's eyes shot to the door as it cracked open and a physician exited, heading their way.

"You're Andrew's parents?" At their nod, he continued. "He's a lucky man. The bullet passed right through without any damage. We want to keep him overnight just for observation. We'll come get you when we have him into a room." He went to walk away but stopped at Emily's voice.

"What was that?"

"Phoebe? How is she?"

"Phoebe?"

Bill spoke up. "Phoebe McBeth, Andrew's wife. She was brought in by air ambulance. Emily and Simon here are her next of kin."

The physician stared at them, then shook his head. "I don't know. I wasn't the one working on her. Let me see what I can find out for you. You're sure she has no other next of kin?"

Bill snorted. "Her former next of kin are the ones responsible for this, and right now, they're in a jail cell awaiting to be charged."

The physician shot Bill a look, taking a step backwards. "I'll be right back." He almost ran from them.

Bill paced, wanting to be at the department as part of the arresting team, but knowing he had to be here. Please, Lord, his heart cried, unable to put into words what he wanted.

Footsteps sounded behind him and he turned, watching another physician approach Emily and Simon. He watched as the physician spoke to them and then turned and walked back to the treatment rooms. He approached as Emily buried her head into her husband's shoulder. Tears sparkled on both their cheeks.

"Simon?" Bill's voice was quiet. He wasn't sure he wanted to hear what they knew.

"Bill. Sit. Just give us a moment please." Simon finally spoke. Then, a moment later, he spoke again. "They took her to surgery, Bill. They have no idea what they'll find. The physician there said she's clinging to life and they would do all they could." A shadow fell across his face. "What do we tell Andrew?"

"We tell him nothing right now. They'll likely have given him strong painkillers that will make him sleep for a while." Bill rested his head back against the wall, his eyes sliding closed. "Do you two need anything?"

Simon shook his head, then spoke. "No, we don't. I told the girls we'd call once we knew something." He pulled out his phone. "They've not met Phoebe yet, you know. We tried to keep as much space between all our girls. It was Andrew's wish. Now, I wish we had ignored that. All three of our girls would get along so well."

Bill's hand found Simon's shoulder and squeezed. "How be I call them for you?"

* * * * *

Hours later, Andrew stirred, grimacing in pain as he moved his leg. His eyes cracked open, and he blinked to clear his eyes. Frowning, he searched the room, not quite sure where he was. A sound to his left drew his eyes that way.

"Drew?"

"Dad?" Andrew's mouth was dry and he had trouble speaking.

"Here's some water, son." Simon held Andrew's head up so he could drink, setting the glass back down on the table.

"Where am I?" Andrew laid back, pain colouring his face.

"You're in the hospital, Drew. You were shot earlier today."

"Shot? How?" Then he remembered. "We were ambushed as we were getting ready to leave. Was anyone else hurt?"

Simon waited, not speaking, his emotions getting the best of him.

"Dad?" Andrew's eyes found his father. "Dad?" Then he sat up abruptly, his eyes roaming the room. "Phoebe? Dad, where's Phoebe?"

Simon pushed Andrew back down, reaching for the medication pump. "You need more pain medications, Andrew. They told me it was time." He watched as Andrew's face clouded. "She's alive and in surgery, Drew."

"In surgery?" Andrew begged his father for more details.

"In surgery. They haven't told us a lot, other than she was shot at least twice."

"How long, Dad?"

Simon shrugged. "Likely around three hours or more. I don't know when they took her in. You've been here for about five."

Andrew dropped his head back. Please, Lord, I can't lose my love. I can't lose my heart.

"Drew?" Simon watched as Andrew slept again and turned, sorrow covering his face. He hadn't wanted to be the one to tell him. He turned as he heard footsteps.

Emily watched her son sleep, then reached for her husband. Simon wrapped her close, not quite sure what to say.

"The girls are here, Simon. I told them I'd come find you." She didn't move, not ready to walk away yet. "I've had word on Phoebe."

Simon watched the tears gather and then trickle down her face. "Emily?"

She turned to look up at him. "She's in ICU, Simon, but they don't expect her to live more than twelve hours. There was extensive bleeding. They've stopped it but feel the damage has been too great. How do we tell him?"

Simon stood, shock shooting through him. "Have you been in touch with Silas?"

"I have. The prayer chain is working every hour. He's opened the prayer room at the church. Prayer is going to be the only thing that gets her through. I haven't told the girls yet. I needed to find Andrew and then you."

Simon nodded, then turned his wife towards the door. "Let's find our girls and then the chapel. I want to see Phoebe as soon as they'll let me."

"Dad? Mom?" Andrew's voice stopped them. "Have you word on Phoebe?"

Emily's hand went to her mouth as she tried to hold back the sobs. Simon pointed her to the door and then stepped back by Andrew. His hand on his son's, he watched, sorrow building inside him.

"Drew. We have. She's in ICU right now." His voice broke and he had to stop speaking.

"Dad?" Andrew sat up, reaching for the blankets. "Take me to her."

"Drew, you're not strong enough."

"I don't care. Either get someone to take me or I'll rip out these lines and find my own way there." Andrew looked past his father to the nurse entering the room. "I need to go up to the ICU, nurse."

"That's what I'm here for, Chief McBeth. An orderly has gone to get a wheelchair for you. I just need to remove these lines. You don't need them now."

Simon stood by the door, watching his son as he pushed his way to the bed where Phoebe lay, reaching out a hand to touch hers.

Andrew stared at Phoebe, seeing the gayness of her face, the faint blue on her lips. He traced her features with his eyes, his heart breaking. He had heard his parents talking before he spoke. He couldn't lose her, not yet. He hadn't been able to keep her safe after all, no matter what he did, or who he found to help him.

His eyes raised to study the monitors, the steady beeping and the hiss and click of the respirator bringing hope. He couldn't pray, he had no words to express how he felt. But he knew God heard his cries.

He balanced himself on his good leg and reached to touch Phoebe's face. It was cold. Oh, Phoebe-love, come back to me. I need you. You're the other half to me.

## Chapter 24

_L_ate that night, Andrew roused from the recliner he was sleeping in. He had adamantly refused to leave Phoebe's side. The physician had finally asked for a chair to be brought in, compassion filling his face as he did so. Andrew had no idea what had roused him, but he studied the form bending over Phoebe.

"What's the problem, nurse? Weren't you just in here?"

The figure stilled, then straightened, turning slightly at Andrew's voice.

"Mary! I should have known it was you. Why?"

Mary turned, anger highlighting her face. "She brought it all down, you know? All our carefully laid plans are ruined because of her."

Andrew was puzzled. "Phoebe?"

"Yes, Phoebe. Why did I ever ask Amos to have you get her out!"

"You know, I'd like to know that as well." Andrew caught the faint shadow of someone behind the curtain covering the entry. "Maybe you could tell me why you set me up."

"You weren't supposed to keep her. You were supposed to bring her to me."

"Why?"

"Because that was how it was supposed to work. Those men she was with were factory workers and they took her to extort money from us. You ruined that. If we had gotten her back, we could have dealt with them."

"Dealt with them, how? By killing them? Where did you go wrong, Mary? How did you get away with lying for so long? I know you never had a husband or family. Why?"

"Because I wanted more and that was the only way someone from outside our town would respect me."

"No one kept you there. But how did you get involved with Phoebe's parents?"

"They approached me years ago, when I first went to work for your parents. I refused, but every six months they kept coming back. I finally agreed to work with them." Anger and fear coloured his face and filled his eyes. "You brought this all down. You and that woman there." Mary pulled out her weapon, pointing it at Phoebe.

"Mary, let's talk about this. You don't want to do that."

Mary turned the weapon to Andrew. "No, you're right. I don't want her. I want you. I hear she's dying anyway. So you might as well join her."

A hand reached for Mary's arm and twisted it behind her, sending her to her knees and the gun spinning away under the bed. A click of handcuffs had Mary secured. Bill stood, his eyes on Andrew.

"Andrew, you okay?"

Andrew nodded, his breath catching I his throat. "I am now. Thank you, Bill. How'd you know she was here?"

"I followed her in. I thought she'd make a try for you two."

A movement on the bed had Andrew up and at Phoebe's side. Bill yanked Mary to her feet and out of the room as nurses rushed in. Andrew was forced to step aside.

The surgeon finally walked to Andrew's side. "We need to take her back to surgery, Andrew. There's some bleeding still going on.  I just viewed the CT images.  My hope is that we can stop it, and you'll have your wife back."

"What are the odds, Doctor?" Andrew's eyes were on Phoebe as the nurses moved her to a stretcher.

"I'm not a betting man, Andrew.  I'm a praying man. My prayer is that she survives. God's will be done."

Andrew watched them leave, then meet his father's eyes.  Simon pushed the wheelchair forward.

"Come, son.  We need to get you back to your bed.  They'll come find us when she's back here."

Andrew nodded, sorrow filling him. Would she really come back to him?  Fear caught at his heart, and then his head bowed. He had to leave her with God.  If He took her home, Andrew would survive, but it would be hard.

✳ ✳ ✳ ✳ ✳

Simon turned from the window in the waiting room as he heard voices in the hallway.  He moved towards Emily, who stared at the woman who entered, a puzzled look on her face.

"Excuse me, do you know where I'd find Andrew McBeth?"

"We're his parents. Andrew can't be disturbed at the moment."

The woman sank to a chair, distraught. "I wanted to talk to him about something."

Emily rose and walked towards the woman, finally sitting beside her, studying her all the while before her face cleared.

"You're Phoebe's mom."

The woman looked up. "Phoebe? Who's she?"

"Andrew's wife and if I'm not mistaken, your daughter?"

The woman sat back, hands flying to her face. "They called her Phoebe? She's alive?"

Emily and Simon shared a look. "She's in surgery right now. Talk to us. Tell us what happened."

Simon looked past them as he heard wheels approached and Andrew appeared in the doorway, his face white with pain and fatigue, disheveled in appearance.

"Mom? Dad?" As he approached, he stopped, his eyes on the woman beside his mother. "You're Lois."

The woman stared at him. "Yes, I am. How did you know?"

"You look so much like Phoebe." His eyes darkened. "Dad, have you heard anything?" When his father shook his head, Andrew sighed, his head dropping. "I was hoping you had."

Lois stared between the three of them, then looked towards the doorway at more footsteps. She rose and went towards the man who appeared, speaking quietly.

Andrew sat, slumped in his chair, his eyes on the floor before he wheeled himself towards the doorway. He stopped as he saw the surgeon approaching him.

Simon watched as Andrew and the surgeon spoke for a few minutes before the surgeon walked away. Andrew slumped even further into his chair, head down, before he scrubbed at his eyes and then his face with the heels of his hands. He turned his chair and headed away from them. Simon touched Emily on her shoulder and then walked after his son, finding him in the chapel. He sat beside him, waiting.

"She's back in ICU, Dad. They could stop the bleeding this time. He thinks she may have a chance now." Andrew swiped at the tears on his face, not wanting his father to see him weeping.

His arm around his son's shoulder, Andrew spoke. "God has been gracious, son. Stay here. I'll go talk to your Mom." He paused, not quite sure how to proceed. "What about the other couple, the ones who may be Phoebe's parents"

Andrew shrugged. "It will be out in the news soon, so I guess it really doesn't matter if they know. I don't want them near her until we confirm they really are her parents."

"Bill had come in just as you left, as had Lily. They'll talk to them for you."

* * * * *

Once more, Andrew stood by Phoebe's bedside, listening to the beeps and hiss and click of the monitors and ventilator. His fingers traced her face, seeing the whiteness of it but no long the gayness underneath or the blueness of her lips. His prayer had been answered so far. Lord, please bring her all the way back. I need my heart healed.

He turned as he heard steps approaching and the curtain whisked back. Richard stood for a moment, watching, before he approached.

"She's better?"

"She is, Richard.  Thank you for your prayers and for all you did for us.  How's Stephen?"

"He's got a headache.  He's also very ticked off that this happened."

Andrew shrugged.  "How could we know what was coming?  Mary hid it well."

"She did.  Your parents worked with her for years and never suspected a thing." Richard turned to stare at the entrance.  "I hear Phoebe's real parents showed up."

Andrew nodded. "Lily's working with them.  It's strange, how this all worked out. She was taken from the church nursery so many years ago.  Her parents never quit searching for her.  The Knights kept her so well hidden not many people saw her.  The eyes would have been a dead giveaway." He reached once more to touch her face, then turned. "Let's go talk, Richard. We need to finish this up, and then I can be with Phoebe."

Richard nodded, his eyes assessing Andrew.  He reached out to steady him as Andrew's eyes slid shut and he crumpled to the floor.

*Epilogue*

Four weeks later, Phoebe sat in the swing on their back deck, eyes tracing the changes the time had brought to the back yard. She smiled. Finally, she was free. She had the answers she had searched for all her life. Her real parents were back in her life as was her sister and two brothers. This family cared about her deeply. They had plans to get together in a couple of weeks. Phoebe had asked for some time to absorb what she had been through. She still moved cautiously, the pain subsiding with time, but still there if she moved wrong or was tired.

Andrew loosened his tie and then ditched his suit coat. He had had to be in court that day and had to dress the part. That he hated, having to dress up. He preferred his jeans and T-shirts. Crossing the deck, he dropped down beside Phoebe, reaching to cradle her close to him.

"Have a good day, love?"

"It's better now you're home. How was court?"

Andrew made some comment, not wanting to waste time talking about someone else. "Where do we go from here, Phoebe?"

She tilted her head to watch him. "What do you mean?"

"I mean, I rushed you into a marriage to protect you. We've been on the run for some many weeks that we really haven't had a chance to get to know each other in a proper manner."

"We've gotten to know and trust and love one another in ways most couples never get." Her hand on his cheek, she leaned in to kiss it. "You are my life, Andrew. Will always be." She sat back, her eyes thoughtful.

"What are you thinking about, love?"

"Andrew, would it be strange if we did a renewal. I know we married and all, but it was just so fast and our families weren't there. Can we do a small wedding, just our families and close friends. Richard and his team, my not-a-cousin-at-all chief, my real family?"

"Phoebe, we can do whatever you want. I think it's a great idea. Has Mom been talking to you?" When she shook her head, he laughed. "I thought she had. She talked to me last night, wanting this for us. She said we needed to do this, to set ourselves on the right "path" as she called it, to have pictures to show our children, if we're so blessed." He stared at Phoebe. "You're blushing, love."

She pushed at him. "I am. That's sounds like a wonderful plan, Andrew. One I never ever thought I would have of my own free will. We need to do some planning. I heard tell Silas wants to have the wedding in two weeks."

Andrew choked on his mouthful of water. "Two weeks? When did he say that?"

"Today when he stopped by." She laid her head on Andrew's shoulder. "God has been good to us, Andrew. We shouldn't have survived what we went through, but we did. I told Silas that God was making beautiful pottery of both of us. He laughed, and then agreed."

Andrew's eyes were on his wife. "And you are the one who is the most beautiful of all." He leaned in for a kiss, then sat back, arms tight around her. "I think we have some planning to do, love, but knowing you, you'll have plans already in motion."

She nodded, her hair brushing his chin. "I do. I need to get together with your Mom and my Mom. I love saying that, but I'm said for all the years I lost with her and the rest of the family."

"God had a plan and purpose for that, love. One we may never ever know about. That's where our faith and trust come in."

The rays of the setting sun traced over them in reds, oranges and pink. The night birds started their choruses and the night insects began singing. Andrew was content. He held all he wanted in the world in his arms.

Dear Readers:

Thank you for picking up the story of Andrew and his love, Phoebe. Quite the adventure Andrew decided to have, now wasn't it? I have been asked where do the stories come from that I write. It is from God. I just write the words He provides.

Andrew became very vocal during Crushed Hope, the fourth book in His Warriors series, demanding that his story just had to be told. I needed a story for him that was a bit different, that showed how brokenness can be made whole. We are all broken in some form. I look at us at clay in the Potter's hands, that God is molding and shaping each one of us to who He wants us to be. It can be a tough and at times hurting journey.

I have loved the image of a potter and clay since I was a child. There is just something about that I can't explain, other than to say seeing a lump of clay turn into something beautiful is a remarkable process.

God bless each one of you as you journey on His path. Remember, He has you in the palms of His hands, molding you to who He wants.

Ronna